# The Coast *of* Good Intentions

# The Coast
# *of* Good Intentions

STORIES

## Michael Byers

*A Mariner Original*
HOUGHTON MIFFLIN COMPANY
BOSTON · NEW YORK  1998

For information about permission to
reproduce selections from this book, write to
Permissions, Houghton Mifflin Company,
215 Park Avenue South, New York,
New York 10003.

*Library of Congress Cataloging-in-Publication Data*
Byers, Michael.
  The coast of good intentions : stories / Michael Byers.
     p. cm.
  "A Mariner original."
  ISBN 0-395-89170-1
  1. Northwest Coast of North America — Social
life and customs — Fiction. 2. Pacific States —
Social life and customs — Fiction.  I. Title.
PS3552.Y42C6 1998
813'.54 — dc21      97-49611 CIP

Printed in the United States of America

Book design by Robert Overholtzer

QUM 10 9 8 7 6 5 4 3 2 1

Most of the stories in this collection have appeared elsewhere,
in slightly different form: "Settled on the Cranberry Coast"
in *The Missouri Review* and *Prize Stories 1995: The O. Henry
Awards;* "Shipmates Down Under" in *American Short Fiction*
and *The Best American Short Stories 1997;* "In Spain, One
Thousand and Three" in *The Writing Path 2, Poetry and Prose
from Writers' Conferences;* "A Fair Trade" in *Prairie Schooner;*
"Wizard" in *The Missouri Review;* "In the Kingdom of Prester
John" in *Indiana Review;* "Dirigibles" in *Glimmer Train.*

FOR MY FAMILY

I OWE THANKS TO MANY PEOPLE:
to Janet Silver, my editor, for her insight
and encouragement; to Timothy Seldes,
my agent, for his diligence and support;
to Stanford, John L'Heureux, and the
Henfield Foundation for precious time;
to Charles Baxter, Nicholas Delbanco,
Eileen Pollack, and Diane Vreuls,
teachers and friends; to John Lofy and
Ryan Harty, friends and careful readers;
and to Susan Hutton, most of all,
for everything, everything.

# Contents

# The Coast *of* Good Intentions

# Settled on the Cranberry Coast

THIS I KNOW: our lives in these towns are slowly improving. When Rosie grew up in the old reservation houses, the roads were dirt and the crab factory still wheezed along, ugly and reeking, and in early summer the factory stayed open all night — it was the only work you could get — and the damp dirty smell of the crab cooking in its steel vats blew off the ocean, all the way to Aberdeen, even farther, for all I knew. I remember driving home from movies in high school, the windows open, the sweet pulp-mill smell of Aberdeen tinged with that distant damp cardboard of Tokeland's cooking crab.

But when the harvest failed fifteen years ago, the state jumped in with some money, and almost at once Tokeland plumped with antique stores and curiosity shops, and the old clapboard hotel became a registered landmark and got a profile in *Sunset*. The Shoalwaters did all right, too — three years ago they sold their fishing rights to the Willapa and voted to put the money into the market, mostly into technology stocks. A lot of them have managed to live off the dividends, and now they buy fishing licenses like the rest of us. Their trawlers are easily the nicest around, you'll notice them moored under the bridge in Aberdeen, the big sleek powerful monsters with aluminum hulls, blue-striped, the new nets, new radar.

Rosie never married, and neither did I. We went to high school together, but we didn't travel in the same crowd. She was half Indian, and she tended to hang with the tough guys, pretty mild by today's standards, I guess — the kids who wore leather jackets, who smoked and overdid the hair gel. Rosie was beautiful, with thick brown shiny hair that reached the middle of her back, but I didn't have a chance at her. She was out of reach entirely, in another world. Her friends, if they drove anything at all, drove pickups instead of cars, and on Friday afternoons they'd motor out to the ocean, pitching and hurtling over the dunes and then speeding down the beach, big V-8s wide open. I envied them, in a way, but I didn't want to be them. Tokeland back then was not a good place to be from. It meant the clapboard shacks for the Indians, and outhouses, and pump wells instead of piped water, all of it on an open spit of land that caught the worst of the ocean winds. Winters, Rosie would say later, the wind would blow all day, all night, until it was part of your soul, an extra function of your body, like your heart, or your breath.

I lost track of Rosie for a while after high school. I went off to college, lived in the East for a few years with a woman I thought I would marry, but things, to make a long story short, didn't work out, and I came home. I took a job teaching high school history in Ocosta and kept at it for twenty-seven years, fishing during the summers and doing some casual carpentry, building rooms onto my house until my back yard was just about gone. Occasionally in the hardware store I'd see someone from Rosie's rough old crowd, most of them prosperous fishermen or at least on their way, the luckiest having inherited their fathers' boats, walking now with the casual swagger of money, wearing designer blue jeans and monogrammed dress shirts. Some of these guys made two hundred thousand dollars in a good year, I knew, and they always had the newest trucks, skinny wives with tousled hair and high heels. They'd recognize me from school, a lot of them, and I'd listen to them worry about their kids sleeping on the beach, the girlfriends and boyfriends, getting into this or that drug, trouble at school, and sometimes they'd ask me for advice. I'd try to tell them their kids would grow out of childhood, just as they themselves had, and privately I wondered why they couldn't see themselves in their children.

When I retired from teaching — packing my classroom with relief, throwing out the battered posters, handing in my teachers' editions for the last time — I found I was restless. Fishing wasn't enough to hold my attention all year. My old women friends were either married or had gone to the dogs in various ways, and a lot had just moved somewhere else. I had some good friends at the high school but I didn't want to linger there, afraid someone might call me a sad old man. On a whim I advertised myself as a carpenter and plumber, but for months my only phone calls were from friends; they'd recognized my name on my sign, they said, and had called to see if it was really me. Oh, it's me, all right, I told them.

Then Rosie called. "I just bought a new house," she said, "and it's a big fucking wreck."

I said, "I used to know you."

"Yes, you did." Her voice was deep and raspy with cigarettes. "Surprise," she said.

There was a second of silence. I said, "So how you been?"

"I've been good."

"Good," I said. "Me too."

"You're as old as me."

"Older," I said. "I think."

"You married?"

"No," I said.

"Divorced?"

"No, nothing. No kids."

"Saw you retired from teaching last year," she said. "Saw you in the paper."

"Yeah. Surprise. Fat." I'd been on stage holding a plaque with the principal and the superintendent, and in the picture my stomach hung out a long, long way in its striped shirt, like a balloon edging through a doorway. I hadn't known I looked quite like that, and staring at the paper I'd felt as though I were seeing myself for the first time in years. "I'm on a diet now," I said. "All that cafeteria food."

She said, "We're none of us getting younger."

I said this was true.

She said, "Are you real busy? I'd like to get started pretty fast."

"I'm not busy."

"I assume you've done this before."

"Oh, yeah," I said. It was a lie. "You working?"

"The state park. I'm a ranger."

"You wear one of those hats?"

"Yeah." She laughed. "So what."

"Never imagined you as the law enforcement type."

"Things change. I'm a legal authority now. I offer no apologies."

"Okay," I said. "Congratulations."

"Thank you," she said.

Twin Harbors State Park sits right on the main roads in and out of the area, hundreds of campsites on both sides of the highway, one side forested and filled with mosquitoes, the other side scrubby and dry, with patches of sand where you pitch your tent in the Scotch broom and shore pine. The campsites sit right alongside one another, children run through the campground, the pit toilets smell. Years ago a friend of mine from college came out to visit me and insisted on camping there, and when I picked him up the next morning the place was littered with beer cans and broken glass, and in the campsite next to his was a sort of blackened skeleton that had been a little pine tree, the soil around it burnt brown. This is where Rosie worked.

But I knew, from working at the high school, that even the dirtiest and least engaging places can grow on you. The high school, a one-story yellow brick building set down in a dirt field, had no windows, supposedly to keep the kids from watching the traffic going by on the highway; the cinderblock hallways were dim and stony. It was an ugly place, institutional. The trees around the edges of the athletic fields had all died from a kind of beetle blight and stood there for years, brown and dry, waiting to fall on the soccer players. But I had my morning car and my thermos of coffee, and there was an easy sort of swinging progression through the years, from holiday to holiday, and the kids were often interested and articulate, and there were lots of good mornings when they were thinking and their hands were raised, or I'd have a sweet kid in a certain period who always understood my jokes, or pretended to. At one point a math teacher named Jack Patani, a little Italian guy, married one of his students, Isabel or Isadora, I could never remember. People were very understanding, for the most part. She was one of the sweet ones who adored him, and who, as he grew to know her, gave him good conversation and a nice young body, and it's hard to argue with that.

Rosie's house sat among rhododendrons right over a little bridge behind the post office, and her back yard ran along the edge of a cranberry bog. She was standing in the driveway, unloading lumber from her pickup. She'd cut her hair short, like a boy's. She wore a white tank top, and her square face held deep wrinkles, like the soft folds in a bag. She stood straight and peered into my car. We shook hands.

She said, "Say it. I look old."

"I look old," I said.

"Very funny."

I said, "You been around all this time? In town, I mean? I mean it's strange we haven't run into each other."

"I keep myself pretty much out of the way." She smiled and her eyes crinkled at the corners. Her eyebrows were thick and black. "Got the water hooked up."

"Okay," I said.

We walked around the corner of the house; her triceps bulged like a weightlifter's. A little rain had started, but she ignored it, put a hand over her eyes. Around the back of the house we could see the beginning of the hills, lit here and there with sun. The alders were in full leaf, and the cranberry bog was a deep russet now in the middle of summer. Down at the end of the road another little house sat, abandoned, its door gaping open as though to breathe, a tree growing through the windows. Somewhere we could hear a tractor. The ocean was a mile away across the highway, invisible, but I could smell it, the salty air.

"See?" she said.

"Nice."

At the back fence, a girl, maybe six years old, was stepping in and out of a plastic wading pool. She was wearing white underpants and no shirt, and her belly hung out like a trucker's. She had Rosie's thick grainy black hair, the same strange overmuscled arms.

"Hannah," Rosie said.

The girl stopped jumping and stepped carefully out of the pool.

"This is Hannah," Rosie said. "My snake in the grass."

"Hello," I said.

Hannah reached up to shake, surprising me, and put her hand solidly in mine — wet and warm, like a little frog in my palm.

"How do you do," I said.

"Walk," said Hannah, and padded back to the pool. "Walk, walk."

"My granddaughter."

"Oh," I said. "Jesus."

We went inside. The house was small and crappy and smelled like mildew. The light fixtures were gone, maybe stolen for scrap, and the cupboards were bashed in; the floor had rotten patches, and the ceiling was a wreck, sagging and stained. The tractor ran noisily along the fence, tending the bogs. "This is what a ranger gets?" I asked.

She said, "I liked the location."

"Well," I said, "so do I."

"It's sort of a shithole right now."

"It might take a while," I said. "It might be a little expensive."

"I know." She was sweeping dust and old nails out of one of the bedrooms. The nails pinged along the floor. "So," she said.

I said, "A granddaughter. Jesus Christ."

She said, "Tell me about it."

At her truck she pulled out a green ranger's shirt and buttoned it, tucked it into her pants. I handed over her ranger's hat — it was stiff, as though it had been in the freezer. "The hat looks good," I said.

"Says you."

"Hi-yo, Silver."

"Right," said Rosie.

Hannah, sitting beside her, said, "Inagada davita, baby."

"Okay. You too."

"She sings," said Rosie. "Inagada davita. Her mother's songs."

"Okay," I said. "That's a little strange, I guess."

Rosie started her truck. Beside her, Hannah sneezed. They waved as they rode off, Rosie glancing behind her as she backed down the driveway.

That afternoon I drove down to Raymond to have lunch with my sister Jodie. She's the principal of the elementary school, but when I found her she was in the teacher's lounge eating a banana and talking on the telephone. She is more or less plump, depending, and her blond hair is most often permed, though that depends on whim, I think: she has thin hair, which she's always hated, and for a while she wore hats everywhere. "Got some news," I said, whispering.

She put down her banana. "Just a second." She held up a fat finger.

"I'll be out here," I said.

I walked into the kindergarten hall, jingling my keys. Scraggly worksheets were stapled to the bulletin boards, and I could smell pee from the bathroom. I looked through the window in a classroom door and saw a teacher, a woman, very young, sitting on the carpeted floor, saying the days of the week. With each word she moved her hands: steepled her fingers together for Tuesday, settled her hands on her shoulders for Wednesday, folded them over her breasts for Thursday. The children's baby faces were set in earnest, their hands moving in grave imitation from shoulder to breast to cheek.

Jodie appeared in the hall, waving to me. Her hem swung around her calves.

"Busy day?"

"Oh." She giggled. "The usual. Parents who don't think their kids should have homework."

We crossed the parking lot to her car, and by the time she got it started I'd told her about Rosie.

"Rosie. Your class. Who had a daughter," she said, tapping her head. "Whose name was Carolyn. Who I think ran off somewhere. I want to say she went to California. I think she worked as an apple picker for a while."

"An apple picker."

"Something. Or strawberries. Something." She shook her head, then laid two fingers on her temple. "I've got too many people up here, they're all starting to look like one another."

"Time to retire."

"I can't afford it. Peter wouldn't like it, anyway." We drove in silence for a minute, then Jodie said, "Does Rosie ever hear from her?"

"From who?"

"Carolyn. Her daughter."

"I don't know," I said. "I just met the woman."

"Just wondering." She pulled into the parking lot of the Lamplighter. "You don't have a problem with that?"

"With what?"

Jodie said, "With Carolyn abandoning a little baby like that. Leaving it with the grandmother."

"You don't know anything," I said. "You don't know a goddamn thing about it."

"Bite my head off," she said.

"You don't."

I followed her into the air conditioning, the dark.

From Rosie that night I learned this: that Carolyn had made it to California, barely, and that Rosie had tracked her down at a strawberry farm, where she was earning two dollars a flat with Hannah, two years old, slung on her back in a shirt. Rosie brought Hannah home for the summer, then for the winter as well, and Carolyn never came to claim her; she wrote twice from Mexico a year later, but on Hannah's fifth birthday her mother was present only in her two letters tacked to Rosie's fridge, in one smiling photograph of her with Hannah on her back, and in Hannah herself, who when asked about her mother remembered nothing, really, just the heat and shady hats, the ghosts of a few songs, and maybe the months of sunshine, and the easy dip and rise of Carolyn picking beans and fruit beneath her.

Since retiring I've put thousands of miles on my car, just driving. It's a way of feeling busy, I suppose. Down to Raymond, inland to Pe Ell and Menlo, down to Vader, sometimes all the way down to Naselle and Skamokawa on the river and the way things used to look around here, the frame houses hanging on the banks, the boathouses on stilts. I can catch Portland radio down there but on the way back up it fades quickly. It's a harmless way to live, more or less, and at least I'm out of the house. And I keep maps: some fairly good ones, with all the little horse trails and logging roads, and a satellite photo, too, which I have tacked to the wall over the bed. In it the sea is a strange dark gray, and the wash from the mouths of the various rivers turns out to be a lighter color, almost a tan, and the roads are laid down like hairs. Houses, too, you can see: the tiniest little white spots, but if you know the roads you can say what's what. The cranberry bogs are square red patches sewn into the flatlands near Tokeland, and Rosie's house is there, too, behind the new brick post office, which sits in the middle of its parking lot like a stone in a puddle. But the thing you notice is the bogs, which stretch for miles, tangled and dense, following the curve of the coastline. Finns, recognizing something familiar in the landscape, built them at the turn of the century, and they're still beautiful things, even from the air.

One afternoon when I was putting up gutters Rosie got out our yearbook and found me in it, combed and chubby. I climbed down from the ladder to look, though actually I'd got the thing out myself weeks ago. "God," she said. "Look at us." She touched the hornrims. "It's a miracle we didn't die laughing at each other."

I leaned over her shoulder. "I still have those glasses," I said, "in case you're wondering." A tractor was churning around the edges of the bog.

Rosie sat on a box and lifted Hannah onto her lap and began flipping the glossy pages. "Your grandmother, Hannah, was not a very good girl."

"Uh oh," said Hannah.

"Oh, I was bad. I didn't do my work in school. I thought it was more important to be with my friends." She glanced at me, then at the tractor, which was coming toward us through the mud.

"Was Eddie one of your friends?"

"Sure he was," Rosie said.

I began picking up clutter — pipe elbows, nail bags, the netting off the bathroom tiles we'd put in that day. "Not a close friend," I said.

"I knew Eddie pretty well," Rosie said. "He had a crush on me."

"Oh yes indeed I did."

The tractor stopped at the gate. The driver, red-haired, stood in the seat and waved, then sat down and gunned the engine. Hannah cringed in Rosie's lap. "Christ," Rosie said.

I walked up to the gate. "Hey," I said.

"Open the gate!" His face was long and prognathic, his front teeth gapped.

"Why?"

He lit a cigarette. "I have to get my mail!"

He gunned the engine again, and I pushed up the latch and swung the gate back. "Thank you very much," said the driver, and halfway to the road he stopped the tractor, stood, dropped his baggy jeans, and peed in a long yellow arc, fifteen or twenty feet, into Rosie's driveway. Then he sat down again and drove off.

"Jesus," I said. "That son of a bitch."

Rosie, smiling, put Hannah gently on the ground and walked to the driveway, where she kicked dust over the mark. "That's the sort of thing I did in school, honey," she called across the yard, and I thought she might have been talking to either of us.

Two weeks later we drove up to Grayland to watch the kite festival. The highway was lined with parked RVs, and a couple hundred people had gathered on the beach. Hannah gave a little gasp when she saw the kites, big fancy ones this year: tandem boxes, double-stringed stunt jobs, black and rippling, and a long rainbow tube, huge and dignified, hanging in the breeze like a blimp.

"Neat," I said, and she shifted toward Rosie and stared out the windshield. She's not used to having a man around, Rosie'd said; she doesn't know what you're going to do. *I* don't know what I'm going to do, I'd said.

"Look at the little black ones," Rosie said.

"I like the rainbow one," Hannah said.

"Good choice." I tried to smile, not make any moves toward her. "The kid knows her kites," I said, and she nodded seriously.

We parked by a hot dog stand. Merle Ingraham, a deputy, was barbecuing hot dogs, wearing an apron. He had mustard in his mustache.

"Merle," I said. "How's things?"

"Keeping my nose clean," he said.

"Actually," I said, and brushed my lip.

He wiped the back of his hand across his mustache. "One too many."

I gestured behind me. "You know Rosie?"

"I think we've met a few times." He nodded at her. "Still working up at the park?"

Rosie said she was.

Merle glanced down at Hannah. "Don't look now," he said to Rosie, "but I think you've got a big dog following you around."

"This is my granddaughter, Hannah. Carolyn's girl."

Merle said, "Carolyn. You don't say."

"Yes."

"Well," said Merle, "she looks like a big dog to me." He stared at her and barked, his boozy eyes red and haggard. "Woof," he said.

Hannah barked back.

"And all this time you thought she was related to you. Been feeding her and everything."

"Woof," Hannah said.

"Your dog," said Merle, "is talking." He handed her a hot dog in a paper napkin; she took it boldly with both hands. I envied the easy way he talked to her, and her smiling for him.

I said, "Who's the guy with the tube kite?"

"I don't know. Some guy." Merle turned the hot dogs. "He's been here before."

We walked over to the man — short, bald, his eyebrows pale and bushy. "Nice kite," I said.

"Thanks."

"This little girl'd love to try it."

He looked at us skeptically. "It's a big one."

"I'll help her out."

He stared into the air.

"Just for a minute," I said.

"That's a thousand-dollar kite," he said. But he handed me the reel, which pulled up and away from me. I knelt down and put my arms around Hannah from behind. She was sweaty and smelled like sun and dirt and meat. The surf rolled over and over itself up the beach. We watched the tube hang majestically above us, spinning in place, like a dream animal. "Three thousand miles," she sang, "miles, miles, miles."

Over the next couple weeks the house got sturdier. I found some old oak boards in my shed and used them to patch the floor. I gutted the kitchen and put in a new fridge, new cupboards, a window over the sink. I was proud of my work — it was quick, cheap, and I didn't make any mistakes, no cuts too short, no crooked wallpaper. The new wall in the kitchen was solid, stronger than the original. Rosie and I worked into the night, the television on in the living room while we put up plasterboard. Sometimes, talking, we woke Hannah, who would come toddling out of Rosie's room and watch. In the television's late blue light her hair shone a sort of steely gray. She wandered over, peered into the joint compound bucket, watched me spread the stuff back and forth. I took a fingerful and laid it in her palm. "Don't eat that."

"I won't." She smelled it, rubbed it between her fingertips.

"We use it to hold pieces of the wall together."

"Glue."

"Right."

She wiped it back into the bucket. "How long until it's done?"

"The house? About a week. Seven days."

Jodie came up one night during that last week with a bottle of wine and a twelve-pack of Henry's. We opened the gate to the cranberry bog and sat down on the grass. The cranberries were pale pink and small, hidden under the creeping leaves. "Here," Rosie said, dropping a handful in my glass. "A touch of elegance."

"Fresh from the bog," I said, and drank deeply. The cranberries rolled around like ball bearings.

"So you're the principal," Rosie said.

"That's right."

"Look out, Hannah," Rosie said. "Eddie's sister is the boss of a school." Hannah said nothing, just crouched at the edge of the bog, collecting the brightest berries she could find.

"I like your house," Jodie said.

"You may thank Eddie for that."

"Yes, you may," I said.

We drank the wine and began on the beer. A mist began wisping in from the ocean, squeezing through the pines and sliding past at eye level. Little tufts settled in the ditches, and scraps hung up in the trees like laundry.

My sister said, "I taught your daughter Carolyn, you know." She was becoming drunk and was making generous gestures. "No. Actually, no, I didn't. I didn't teach her. What am I saying? But I remember her. More or less."

"She didn't get too far," Rosie said.

"No, I remember that. A beautiful girl, though. Very pretty." Jodie opened another beer. "A very pretty girl."

"Thank you."

"You're welcome."

"I don't think we have to worry about seeing her around here any time soon," Rosie said.

Jodie nodded. "Well," she said.

"She is no longer a part of our lives," Rosie said, and something about the way she said *our* made us all look over at Hannah, who lay picking at the grass. I could imagine moving in with these two, sure, sleeping on the sofa at first — an urge to lend a hand, I suppose, to take on this little family — though they seemed whole there, at the edge of the bog, as if that *our* had sealed them off from us somehow. Rosie wore a strange expression, not of wonder, exactly, which you'll see on new mothers, but something closer to acceptance, and regret. I was drunk but not drunk enough to say what I wanted, that we don't live our lives so much as come to them, as different people and things collect mysteriously around us. I felt as though I were coming to Rosie and Hannah, easing my way toward them.

"Don't let it bother you," Rosie said, leaning, her hand on my thigh. "She's not even something I think about anymore. She's gone, gone, gone. And now here's Eddie." She kissed me on the cheek. "Am I drunk?" she asked. Her eyes were bright.

"Probably."

"Oh, good." She rubbed her face with her palms. "Don't even think about her," she said. "No point anymore." I sat, holding my beer. What was she imagining? Pheasants in the migrants' shacks, the mattresses that swelled with dew and rain between seasons? "No point," she said. Her lowered voice, the finality of it, and I imagined the orchards hanging full of fruit, a faceless Carolyn lost in the trees.

I spent the night on Rosie's sofa and woke up early, not sick exactly but with the feeling that a wind was blowing through my head, that I had created a few vacancies upstairs. I made coffee and sat on the front porch, facing the back of the post office. The flagpole was still empty; it was Saturday. The yard was littered with wood scraps. I sat there, retired teacher, gut on my lap, plaster dust all over my pants.

After a while, Hannah walked out on the porch with a bowl of cereal. "Good morning," I said.

She looked at me and ate her cereal.

"Want to go to Aberdeen with me today?"

"If you go," she sang, "to San Francisco." She stopped, ate another spoonful, sat down next to me.

"You like those hippie songs," I said.

She shrugged.

I said, "I have to go buy some radiators, I was wondering if you want to come along."

"How long is that?"

"How long is what?"

"The trip," she said.

"Twenty minutes. We won't be gone more than an hour." I noticed the delicate point of her chin, like Rosie's chin.

"Okay," she said.

"Good," I said. "Saddle up."

I left a note for Rosie: *Gone for radiators with Big Dog.*

She climbed into the car by herself, and I leaned over to point out her seatbelt, but she grabbed the two ends and clicked them together. I could think of nothing to say. Her presence was palpable, her thick meaty smell. We were both a little tense. "We could get you an ice cream cone there," I said, and then remembered it was only eight in the morning. "Or maybe some pancakes."

She folded her hands in her lap and stared straight ahead, at the glove compartment.

"Remember where we're going?"

"Aberdeen."

"The kid has a memory," I said.

She said, "I wasn't sleepy last night."

"Maybe you could nap now."

"I'm not sleepy now, either."

"You could try."

She closed her eyes, her hands clasped rigidly in her lap.

"Jesus, relax," I said, but she didn't move.

I drove quickly, my window cracked open. What had Jack Patani said? He'd married Isabel, Isadora, to give himself a few more good times. Still happy together, those two, and he'd had several nice years, was looking at many more. I admitted to myself, then — I allowed myself to think, then, for the first time, about marrying Rosie. I still hardly knew her at all.

Over the bridge in Aberdeen I nudged Hannah. She shifted a little in her seat, but she was asleep, her hands still clasped together.

"Hannah," I said. But she was out like a light.

She was still asleep when we parked, so I walked around to her door, unbuckled her seatbelt, and lifted her against my shoulder. I carried her inside, the lopsided sack of her against me. Around us stretched miles of lumber and pipes, and somewhere I heard a saw whining, but she didn't wake up; and as I walked through the aisles she spread her arms, her fat arms, to hold my neck, and I imagined that she remembered this strolling motion, and that more than any rocking could, or singing, it soothed her. I talked to the salesmen, and I handed over my wallet. Outside, it was raining, and I waited under a metal overhang. She slept as they loaded the radiators, clanking, into the trunk of my car, one after the other — they angled out awkwardly, and I had a flag tied on — and then I was alone with Hannah in the parking lot, waiting for the rain to stop, and I stood watching the rain come down over the river, over the ships and bridges, and over the highway home. I smoothed her hair with my hand, her head perfectly round against my shoulder, and I stood — I was on the verge of something, I could feel it — and I just waited there, listening to her easy, settled breathing.

# Shipmates Down Under

**M**Y DAUGHTER Nadia was sitting up in bed, and she looked perturbed, as if someone had told her a joke she hadn't understood. She had books arrayed around her like brochures, but she wasn't reading. This was my youngest child, six years old and smart as a firecracker. Her room smelled thick, a musty fog of feet and dirty pajamas, and her plastic dolls lay dismembered here and there on the carpet, arms missing, plastic heads scattered like nuts. "Looks like a war zone," I said.

She squinted at me. "Bluh."

I put a palm on her forehead. "Geez, Najee, you're really hot."

"I have a fever."

"You sure do." I hugged her gently. She was wet and limp as a weed.

"Edith kept giving me apple juice," she said.

"You feel all right?"

"No." She scowled at me. "I feel sick."

"Feel like you're about to yurk?"

"I almost did at school," she said. "Then I fell asleep in class and I had these weird dreams."

"What of?"

"There were all these lines," she said. She wiggled her fat fingers and squinted. "And I had to keep track of all the lines going back and forth, and they kept cutting in half, and I couldn't wake up. And Edith had to pick me up, and I almost yurked in the car."

There were crusts in the corners of her eyes, and she plucked at them.

"Edith drove?"

"Yes."

"Oog," I said. Edith was our housekeeper, not good with the car.

"It was okay," Nadia said.

"I really don't like Edith's driving," I said.

"I think it's fun."

"It gives me nightmares," I said.

"Well, we almost ran over a dog," Nadia said, judiciously.

For six years Nadia had been a perfect pink baby, blessed with a preternatural happiness that I occasionally found unnerving. Who should be as happy as this? At times I thought she was putting on a baby's determined act for us, ignoring her brother Ted, who threw dead beetles in her crib (Harriet and I had read about these things) and later made Nadia his personal slave — *get me oranges, get me raisin bread, get me dried peaches* — while he watched basketball games or built his tremulous towers of blocks. Nadia no longer did these things for Ted, thank God — it makes you nervous, watching your kids naturally re-enacting the grimmest parts of history — but neither did she hold a grudge against him. She was happy to be here, it seemed, and, as if in reward, she was beautiful, very much resembling my wife with her pale snowy skin and dark wavy hair, and she had, like Harriet, a thick spray of freckles beneath her eyes and over the fine bridge of her nose. You sat her on her rump on the counter like sculpture and she beamed, pushing her hair out of her eyes.

Ted, my young man, my acolyte, had been different, a difficult baby, small and wormy. He'd squirm out of our hands when we picked him up, or he'd lie in his crib screaming like a seagull. At nine, now, he was suddenly serious about being my son — he'd recently decided to be a doctor, too, a geneticist, like me. *I want to help people,* he'd said carefully, watching me, and he wanted to know all about genetics, so in the evenings we'd take out the yellow pad and go AGCTCGGT, TCGAGCCA, amino acids, ionic bonding, mRNA, on and on. We were conspirators, men together. He never let on when he was confused — he was too proud — but I'd see his green eyes glaze over and

I'd want to pull back from him, stop inflicting myself on him. But he insisted, and we went on, maybe out of pride on my part, or fear of embarrassing him, and we sat elbow to elbow in the bright kitchen and worked it through — mutations, chromosomal breakages, Turner's, Cri du Chat, this basic damage done so easily, unintended.

I was cooking when Harriet came home from work. She had the *Times* rolled up in her hand, and she waved it at me, once, and sat at the dining room table, her long pink skirt settling around her like a parachute.

"Well hello," I said.

She rattled the newspaper. "Mumph," she said.

"Mumph yourself."

My wife saw dying kids every day, kids with cancer or cystic fibrosis, and she often had to inspect the bodies of stillborn babies, dead collodions whose yellow skin had cracked like parchment, anencephalics born flatheaded, their hair thick and medieval. This was her specialty, pediatric genetics, a grim business, and she saw every week in clinic a series of freakish, broken children, the old products of witchcraft and comets, of horrible sins and longings, though sometimes I think our explanations these days don't make much more sense: cosmic rays? Pesticides? Genetic disposition? Occasionally I found Harriet staring off over dinner, her eyes fixed in the mirror behind the table, entranced by us all, by our hands and arms equal in number, and nimble; by our foreheads, high and clear.

So I stayed in the kitchen, letting her read the paper, stirring the chili with a long wooden spoon.

When she came back in I said, "Nadia's got a fever."

"She does? How high?"

"Highish," I said. "I haven't checked."

Harriet took her wine glass and started for the stairs. She glared at me. "Jesus, Alvin, you know that fucking *Edith* never calls me. I'd think at least *you'd* tell me."

"I just did," I said, but she was gone.

Often lately I had been unable to predict Harriet's moods, something I'd always been good at — in fact, I'd once been so good at predicting them that it used to surprise me, mild precognitions that felt very much like dreaming, in which I'd known, as in a dream, what Harriet would be feeling. I'd have baths ready for her, and I'd call her at odd hours during the day: *How did you know?* And this sort of prescience made her fall for me, I think, when we were both interns, both haggard and sleep-deprived, tossing on thin blue cots in big bright rooms. But now Harriet's moods seemed to me volatile and dangerous, not so much changing as crushing one another in succession, and it made me nervous; I was afraid that one imprecise word would enrage her, irrationally. She'd curse me; I'd curse her; we threw words at each other. How had we come to this? She was, of course, under great strain at work, she needed a break — and, in fact, in ten days we were all going to Australia, to Perth, the city where I'd spent the first ten years of my life. I hadn't been back, and I was excited, two weeks at the big Normandy Hotel, renovated now, according to the brochures, rid of its sailors and prostitutes.

When Harriet came downstairs her wine glass was empty. "A hundred and three," she said.

"Ack."

"I'm pissed off, Alvin."

"I know." I turned off the burner.

"I specifically asked her to call us when the kids get sick."

"So fire her," I said. "If you want."

"If *I* want?" she said. "Why me? I don't want to fire her. We had enough trouble finding her in the first place."

"Or I could. Whatever."

"I don't think you're even worried about her." Harriet peered at me, her long Irish nose aimed like a saber.

"About Nadia?"

"Yes, about Nadia."

"Of course I am," I said. "But kids get sick."

But awake in bed that night, with Harriet slim and silent under the quilt next to me, I spun out a series of fantasies, an old gray spider sick with worry: Nadia's fever didn't break, and she grew sicker and sicker; she fainted, red-faced and delirious, and she fell down the stairs, her head banging like a wooden shoe. The fever became a speckle of

chicken pox, then viral meningitis, then the first gray augur of leuke-
mia. Jets passed over the house, blinking across the Plexiglas skylight,
and my mind moved relentlessly into a number of congested futures.
Why do we torture ourselves with these things? We're intrigued by
pain, I suppose, by the possibilities of submission it offers. Sickness
was once a demon we let in willingly, which meant that the sick were
sick willingly, by their own hands, punishing themselves, and this is at
least a bit true, I think.

So I got out of bed and put on my robe. The room extended in
darkness, the sloped walls. Our big bedroom was at the peaked top of
the house — we had the whole third floor to ourselves — and tonight
the windows rattled and little individual gusts went tossing along the
floor like loose paper. On the way downstairs I touched the hard plaster walls with my palms. It was ten minutes to midnight.

I went to Nadia's room. She was asleep on top of the sheets. The
room was dark, but around the edges of the room I could sense the
bumpy shapes of her stuffed animals, and then, as I approached her
bed, she turned and stared straight at me, and she frightened me —
the whites of her eyes glowed like eggs, and her hair was plastered
against her head. I turned on the lamp, and she rolled away like a dog.
I slipped the thermometer under her tongue and held her round wet
head in my hands. She rolled her cheek against my palm. She was hot
and shivering, and I imagined the long senseless wiry lines dividing,
halving and multiplying, relentless.

Her fever was a hundred and two. I got her a glass of water, which
she drank, slowly, and I took a washcloth from the bathroom rack,
wet it in the sink, and wiped her face and ears and her rounded
forehead, the hollow in her neck. "Yodey yode," she said, scowling.

"Yodey yodey," I said, daubing at her eyes.

"Rings in reedoreed."

"Yes indeedy deed," I said. She winced when I rubbed her nose.

She was still shivering, so I tucked her beneath the sheet and pulled
the blankets over her shoulders. She said, "Finish time."

For a while I sat with her, listening to the house — it creaked and
popped in the wind as if loosing its hawsers — until it subsided again,
when I said, "If you need anything, just yell, and I'll come down for
you," and she nodded weakly. I kissed her salty cheek and left the

room, but I left her door open so we could hear her, though now she was deep in the blankets, calm, her face away from the door, her black hair flying behind her on the pillow like a small dark flag.

Next door, Ted's light was on. I knocked once and whispered, "Can I come in?"

There was a rustle of bedclothes. "Sure," he said.

He was sitting up in bed, reading. His long pale arms reached, hairless and smooth, across the blankets. His room was spare and clean. An empty white desk stood by the windows, and his books were aligned perfectly in the shelves. He was neat as always, tidy as a curate, a penitent. Tomorrow's clothes sat folded on the desktop.

"How's Nadia?" he asked.

"Still feverish."

"Mom said she has to go to the hospital."

"Maybe tomorrow, if she doesn't get better." And now I felt the house warm a little, felt us inhabiting it as a family — how else can I describe the feeling I have with my son? If I know anything about love, it's his doing. I said, "You should be asleep."

"I don't have school tomorrow."

"Yeah, it's late, though."

"Ten minutes," he said.

"What're you reading?"

He tipped the book, a ratty paperback: *Danny Dunn and the Voice from Space.*

"You've read that before."

"A couple times," Ted said.

"What's it about?"

"There's these two boys, and this girl, and they have a professor friend, and they make contact with an alien race with a radio telescope. It's sort of science fiction."

"What do the aliens have to say?"

"Well, what they do is send a picture of themselves. And then later they send more, at the end, but that's where the book ends, unfortunately."

This depressed me; Nadia had read that book, too, at six, and I didn't want Ted to fall behind. "Let me recommend something," I said. I walked to Ted's bookshelf. "It's about Australia."

"Are you in it?"

"No," I said, scanning the shelves. "But I used to read it over and over."

"What's it called?"

"It's called *Shipmates Down Under*. It's got a green cover."

Ted sat up straighter in bed.

I found it, pulled it out, and sat at the foot of his bed. "You should read this before we go."

"What's it about?" He shrugged in his pajamas.

"Well, it's about this boy whose name is Lionel and his friend Ewing, and they stow away on a pirate ship that's going to India or someplace, and they go to this emir's castle, this big old castle in the jungle, and that's where they have their adventures."

Ted rubbed his nose. He was listening, as he always listened to me: intently, seriously, as if studying for a role.

"So." I opened the book to the middle and read aloud, whispering: "'*At long last, night fell upon the weary boys, and they slept deep in the hold, huddled close to each other for the warmth their bodies gave, while above them the splendid ship creaked and shuddered, crashing through the salty main. The sea splashed against the bulwarks of the mighty ship, and spray hissed past their heads.*' They're stowing away," I said.

"Mm-hm."

"'*Late at night Lionel woke, believing he felt something climbing over his legs and he shouted out, "Get off!" and shook his legs with all his might. But he felt nothing more and thought perhaps he had been dreaming. In the darkness of the hold he could see only the colours of black and grey, and these melted into one another a few feet from his eyes. Perhaps it had been a rat. He knew rats lived in the holds of ships, eating the stores of grain and whatever else they could find. Slowly the ship rocked him back to sleep.*'"

"They're going to India?"

"Yep."

"Do they have any money?"

"No," I said, "I don't think so."

"How're they going to eat?"

"Well, it's an adventure. They don't know how it's going to turn out."

"Sounds like they're pretty stupid to me."

"Well, maybe so."

"They should plan things out better," he said. "What if they starved?"

"I guess so," I said. "But I liked it because they lived in Perth, so I could pretend it was about me."

"Oh."

"Actually, I had a friend in Perth named Lionel, but I don't think he ever read it."

"Why not?"

"I don't know."

He looked at me levelly. "I'll read it after this," he said, and put it neatly beside him, by his clock radio. He listened to talk stations and to oldies, and as I left his room he turned the radio back on, very low, a measured murmur. Of course I love my children, and I love Ted and his eccentricities, his fierce, perverse maturity, and I loathe parents who condescend to their children, or who think any ill of them at all, but I do find Ted a little strange; he is so principled and controlled. He had already packed for Australia; he had a journal and a pencil tucked in the side pocket of his suitcase, and I expected him to record our travel times, and meals, and mileage. It is, I think, one of the many discoveries of parenthood, that you can love your children differently — not more or less, but differently.

Upstairs in our sloped room Harriet was sleeping on her back, as if contemplating the sky through the skylight. And once in bed I did feel calm again, more certain of a single, easy future. I believed Nadia would be better tomorrow, and when we flew out next Saturday I would sit beside her and she'd stare out the airplane window as the earth dropped away. Now I too stared up, out through the skylight at the blinking jets, and I heard our old house creak, and I imagined it tipping like a ship, or maybe just like an old house sailing into the night, its four stowaways tucked safely in.

I woke alone the next morning. Through the skylight I saw blue sky, high white clouds, a cold, windy winter day. Harriet was gone. Her side of the bed was already made. Downstairs, Harriet and Ted were crouched in their robes on Nadia's bed, and Harriet was whipping the thermometer back and forth with her wrist. "A hundred and four," she said.

Nadia was asleep, her head lolling on the pillow. I felt her forehead: papery and rough, as if her skin were being cured. Her mouth was open.

"She's been throwing up." In the bottom of the red bowl — Harriet passed it to me — was a pool of what looked like thick stringy water. It smelled sour and strong, an alchemist's condensation of sickness. "Nice," I said. Harriet swirled the vomit once, slowly, as if reading a fortune.

Ted said, "She doesn't look too good."

"No, she doesn't."

Harriet fluffed her hair and stood, then moved briskly, her heels thumping away down the hall. She poured the vomit into the toilet and flushed it down.

Nadia didn't wake up for another hour — Ted sat by her, reading his book on his lap and feeling her forehead with his pale, narrow palms — and then she woke up and vomited a thin green fluid on the carpet, as if she'd been eating grass. "Dad!" Ted called, still in his blue pajamas, and Harriet and I came running up the stairs, and with a gathering sense of dread, a sense of *This is real, this is no dream*, I wiped her white face and lifted her gently against my shoulder and walked downstairs. She was soft and pliant; she seemed to have no bones at all; her head rolled back and forth as I stepped carefully down, down, down, past the pictures, past the coat rack, out into the world. At the curb I buckled her into the back seat, pulling the belt tight over her hips. She put her head back and began talking. "Over in the end," she said, sighing delicately. "Tall and tall and tall. And the mag's around."

"She's delirious," Harriet said, calmly. She reached back and patted Nadia's hair.

"You don't seem too concerned," I said.

"No, neither do you."

Nadia said, "Ohzy ohzy ohz."

Harriet took a breath and said, "I had a kid last week who was babbling like that. Not a fever, just a drug reaction."

"Oh?"

"Turned out his parents were Swedish."

I whipped the car around a corner, clipping bushes. "An accent."

"No, the kid was speaking Swedish. His crib language."

"No kidding." I reached my hand back and groped for Nadia's head. It felt loose, dry, inhuman. "Was he all right?"

"Oh, sure." She smiled. "We just switched his medicine."

The university hospital is a white sprawling building, set back in trees by the lake. In the marble lobby, under a huge dry ficus, Harriet clipped her black nameplate to her shirt. "I'll check her in," she said, and disappeared around a corner. Nadia babbled softly into my ear, telling me peculiar secrets, a string of letters, random and tangled. "Bobido medee," she said. "Winda beena." The lobby was bright with Christmas music, and a decorated tree loomed in the corner, gifts spread beneath it. Patients parted and hobbled along, a little veterans' parade. There were two boys in aluminum wheelchairs and a man with a ball of gauze where one eye should have been, and a bald woman walking out slowly to see the parking lot. A gold fountain sprayed softly in the middle of the lobby. I shifted Nadia's weight on my shoulder; she was sleeping again. I checked her back to be sure she was breathing, and she was, deeply and evenly, her round warm back rising like a loaf of bread in my hand. "Najee," I said. And if I'd turned around, taken her away from this harmful place, walked out into the sunny, windy parking lot? Hell to pay, of course. Unforgivable.

Nadia's room had sky-blue walls and reading lamps by the beds, not bad as hospital rooms go. The windows looked down from a great height on Portage Bay and the marina and the university. "Nice view," I said. There was a boy in the other bed, a fat boy with a crew cut, and he turned and looked at the view for a long time, as if he hadn't noticed it before. I lay Nadia gently on the white narrow bed.

"There'll be a nurse in a minute," Harriet said.

I tucked Nadia's legs beneath the sheet.

"I'm just going to run her blood down to the lab," Harriet said. "Make sure there's nothing really wrong with her."

She wasn't supposed to do that, but I didn't say anything, and neither, I suspected, would anyone else. From the wall cabinet she took a blood vial, tore the flat paper off a needle, and fitted the two together; then she gently arranged Nadia's arm, turning it upside down as she would a piece of chicken. "Just a little sting," she said, and delicately pierced Nadia's arm. Nadia didn't stir. Harriet drew blood, the needle in and out in a second, no mark at all, and held the vial to the light as if it were a jewel, a red, dark charm. "The nurse'll get an IV going," she said, and charged out the door, holding the vial in her fist.

Nadia sighed once and rolled over on her stomach, wincing into her thin pillow.

"What's wrong with her?" the fat boy asked. His leg was elevated on a frame beneath the sheet.

"Ssh," I said. "Don't wake her up."

"Sorry."

"That's all right." I walked to his bed. His big body mounded up like a balloon. "What happened to your leg?"

"I broke it falling off a horse."

"Ouch."

"Yeah. And the horse rolled over on me."

"Oof." I lifted the sheet. His knee was soft and purple, a big fleshy eggplant, and his shin was encased in a plaster cast.

"I got four pins put in."

"Congratulations."

"It hurts," the fat boy said.

"I bet it does."

"Are you my new doctor?"

"No, but I'm *a* doctor," I said. "Sort of. I do research. That's my daughter, Nadia. She'll probably be here a couple days."

"What's wrong with her?"

"She's got a fever that won't go down."

He snorted.

"A fever can be very dangerous if it doesn't go down by itself. She can't keep anything in her stomach. She keeps throwing up."

"That's a little gross."

"What's your name?"

"Dustin."

"She's Nadia."

Then Harriet came in and said, "There isn't a nurse on this whole goddamn floor."

"This soldier over here's got a busted leg," I said. "Horse rolled on him when he was charging the enemy bunker."

Harriet smiled wanly. "I'm going to go find someone," she said, and disappeared.

"Is *that* the doctor?" Dustin asked.

"That is the doctor," I said, as the door sighed shut.

I drove home alone. I found Ted in the kitchen in my big wicker chair, still wearing his pajamas. He was drinking a cup of coffee and reading *Shipmates Down Under.* "Hey!" I said. "Good book."

"Where's Mom?"

"Taking care of business," I said. "Nadia's the same. She'll be fine." It seemed right to say that. I mean, I didn't feel as if I was lying. We were, after all, taking extreme measures, precautions — more to make sure we could all go to Australia on time than anything else, more for us than for her. Six days? Surely she'd be better in six days.

"I like this book," Ted said. He scratched his armpit. "I like their school."

"That's a real school, you know, in Perth. The Palmer School. For rich kids."

"You were rich."

"We were definitely not rich," I said.

He felt his thick hair and said, "Did people really talk like this?"

"Like what." I bent over the book, put my hands on his shoulders.

"Like, 'This is a gosh-awful bore.'" He was on page eight.

"No. At least no one I knew did. I didn't."

"What'd you talk like?"

"Me? I don't know. We used to say things were *shorey.*"

"Shorey?"

"It meant sort of, like, cool."

"Where'd that come from?"

"I don't know. We also used to say *decent.* If something was great, we called it decent."

"Uh-huh." Ted turned back to the book.

"So," I said. But he was gone, lost in it.

I made myself a cup of coffee and went upstairs. There, I straightened my half of the bed and sat down at my desk. She'll be fine, I thought; of course she'll be fine. Harriet will call. From my desk I could see the lake, gray and cold, and here and there I could see red

Christmas lights strung on porches, swinging in the breeze, and, across the lake, the soft, mounded hills of Bellevue, the huge waterfront houses, the yachts, the long, precarious docks. To distract myself, I suppose, I too began to read.

*Gene* had a special issue on skin disorders, which made for gruesome reading — children turned inside out or split open, or their legs patchy with blisters — not my field anyway, so I could put it down without professional guilt. *Genetics* was full of the Human Genome Project, the vast mapping of the human coastline, with landmarks along the way, here lupus, here polydactyly, the tiny jeweled inlets where things were kept: the Bay of Eyelashes, the Strait of the Brow, the Islands of the Hands, though it would take years to get all the way around, decades, and I'd read about most of it elsewhere. But *National Genetics Review* had published a paper on Fatal Familial Insomnia, one of my favorite diseases, a syndrome in which patients, around the age of forty, slowly and irrevocably lost the ability to sleep. The patients could take years to die, losing ground gradually to madness, and as the disease progressed they showed a handful of bizarre symptoms — ataxia, amnesia, temporal disorientation, forgetting who and where and when they were, sleepless — and at the very end they told long, fabulous lies: they were spies for unimaginably powerful kings, or they had designed machines that could cure cancer or end hunger or destroy the world — and they insisted on these ideas as madmen do, with utter sincerity. *Confabulation* was the technical term, a pleasant-sounding word that suggested to me a velvet painting: rainbows and flying unicorns and staircases spiraling into the clouds, a complete, fanciful realm where the world could be told and retold. The whole thing was a sort of horror story, and afterward I sat uneasily at my desk, imagining the advance scouts of age and dementia, my mind leaking slowly away through my ears, my pacing, sick and doomed, through the windy house, coming to know the remotest corners of the night. But of course it was very rare, and inherited to boot.

So the morning passed, and at noon I went downstairs. Ted was still sitting at the kitchen table in his pajamas. "You haven't moved," I said.

"Still reading."

"You like it?"

"Yeah. They're in Ceylon now. Which I couldn't figure out where they were, but I looked it up and figured out it's Sri Lanka."

"Have you got to the emir's palace?"

"No. They're walking around some town."

"The palace is my favorite part," I said.

"They're still talking weird." He smiled down at the table.

"The way I used to."

"You still talk weird."

"Ha ha."

"You do," he said. "*Leever. Rahther.*"

"Listen, smart guy. I've been talking since before you were born."

He laughed.

"At least I don't talk like those guys. If we'd known anyone who talked like that we'd have beat the crap out of him."

He laughed again.

The phone rang. It was Harriet. "Alvin," she said. "She spiked at a hundred and four, two hours ago, and now she's back down to a hundred and two. It looks like some sort of throat infection, but it's weird. It's not in her tonsils. It's in her tongue and in her palate. She might need to have her adenoids out."

"Her palate's infected?"

"Well, maybe. It's weird."

"Weird how?"

"I've just never seen it before. She still can't keep anything down."

"She awake?"

"Sometimes."

"She scared?"

"A little. She doesn't know exactly where she is yet."

"You coming home?"

"Maybe. Maybe tonight. I want to see how she is. I might end up staying."

"Well. Say hello for me," I said, gently.

"I will." She cleared her throat. "She'll be okay," she said, and she was gentle, too, unusually so.

When I hung up, Ted asked, "When's she coming home?" He was hopeful, honest; we were here together, and he liked that, he liked having me to himself, and I liked it too.

I said, "Couple days, probably. She has a throat infection."

"I'm excited about Australia now," he said.

"Really? Well, good."

"We might not go, though, right." He examined his hands. "If Nadia doesn't get better."

"That's right," I said. "We might not."

"I figured."

"We'll probably go."

"I'd like to see your house."

"You would?"

"You think it's still there?"

"Oh," I said, beaming, "it's probably still around."

"Can we go see it?"

"Sure."

"What'd it look like?"

"Well, it was white when we lived in it, and it had a concrete porch and a walled-in yard. I had a bedroom in back I shared with my sister."

"Did you have any friends?"

"Sure. Australian friends, you mean?"

"Yeah."

"Sure. I was telling you about that guy Lionel. We didn't go to any special school or anything. It was just the elementary school. Primary school." I smiled. "I'm excited too, if you can't tell."

"Yeah." Ted gave a wry grin.

"You think I'm being silly?"

"No."

"Did I ever tell you about the streetcars?"

"Just about a billion times."

"We used to have a picnic on Christmas morning," I said. "The seasons are reversed down there, you know. We'd have turkey sand-wiches and go out to the beach."

"You told me that, too," Ted said.

So I left my son alone, reading in the kitchen, and when I was halfway up the stairs I called down, "I want a book report on my desk by tomorrow!" — and I remembered the rotten old white palace, deep in the jungle, where, through a tangle of vines, the boys had spied a golden pool, and where they had slept, soundly, and awakened to find that the palace monkeys had gathered for them heaps of gleaming fruit, papayas and bananas and thick, rich breadfruit, and I remembered the monkeys sitting at a respectful distance, off in the high white niches and alcoves of the walls.

When Harriet clomped up the stairs that night I was already in bed.

"You look cozy," she said, and threw down her backpack.

"How's the kid?"

She sighed. "Okay. She had another spike this afternoon at a hundred and three, but when I left she was at a hundred and two. It's normal, more or less. Stubborn."

"You came home, though."

"She's okay. I told her I'd be back in the morning. She likes the nurse."

"That fat kid talk to her? Dustin?"

"Ugh."

"Seemed nice enough," I said.

"He was reading a pornographic comic book."

"No he wasn't," I said.

"He was, Alvin."

"Batwoman's pretty hot these days."

"Batwoman doesn't wear garters and walk around naked on a glass table."

"Huh," I said. "No."

"So I gave him the evil eye," Harriet said.

"I know the feeling."

"I should've taken it away from him."

"It's none of your business," I said.

"What if he decides to limp over and practice on Nadia?"

I closed my eyes and got deeper under the quilt. "Christ, Harriet. Don't say that."

"I bet you used all the bathwater."

"No."

"You're always inconsiderate with the water," she said.

"Oh, shit," I said. "I am not."

She ran the tub, and I began to fall asleep.

Then she said, "Did you ever go out to the outback?"

"Once or twice."

"What's it like?"

"Oh . . ." There'd been a bus trip, but I hardly remembered it; nor did I feel like remembering it at the moment, or talking to her about it. "Like Nevada, but prettier."

"Can we go? Is it a kind of day-trip arrangement?"

"Maybe a couple days."

"Would you want to do that?"

"Sure," I said.

She splashed away for a minute, then said, "Nadia says hello."

"Hello," I said, and smiled in the dark.

When we arrived at the hospital the next morning Nadia had a rash below her nostrils, like red silt spilling from a river's mouth. She was breathing shallowly, and her skin was pale. The plastic IV tube snaked away, a second umbilicus.

"What the hell." I touched her rash. She was still asleep.

"I don't know," Harriet said. "That's very strange."

"She was talking last night," Dustin said.

"I'm going to find somebody," Harriet said, and left.

Dustin said, "She wasn't making any sense."

I adjusted the blankets. The sheet by her head was stained orange.

"She was all, like, talkative. Sounded like she was having a conversation."

I propped her up with pillows. Her head rolled, frighteningly loose. "She was delirious," I said. "She didn't know where she was. That happens a lot when people have fevers."

"Sounded like she was crazy."

"She's not crazy."

"Pretty annoying if you ask me."

"How about you just quiet down over there, kiddo," I said.

"Why?"

"Because."

"You think she's going to die?"

"Watch your mouth," I said.

"Huh."

Nadia's lips were chapped and cracked, and I sat at her bedside and watched them roll against each other — there were words in there, I thought. But she said nothing, nothing I could hear.

After work Monday night I walked back down through the dark wintertime campus to the hospital — Christmas lights hung in the fir trees up and down Rainier Vista, and it was sprinkling, and there were students hurrying off to exams — and I went upstairs to Nadia's room, ducking past the hairy-armed attendants pushing their shiny silver carts full of dinner. Nadia was asleep and looked a little better — her hair had been combed and washed — but the rash had spread to her nose and cheeks and had started around her eyes, like a raccoon's mask. I touched it: it was springy, raised, tender. She winced in her sleep and turned away. I pulled up a chair.

"That girl's looking weird," Dustin said. He was watching television — a stock car race — holding the remote in front of him like an offering. "She'd better not be contagious, that's all I've got to say."

"She's not contagious," I said, though I wasn't sure. Harriet was around somewhere. Her pink backpack was on the side table.

"She woke up today around lunchtime," Dustin said.

"Really? Good."

"Yeah, for like six minutes. She didn't want to watch TV."

"Well, she's not feeling so good."

"The doctor was in here a lot, too. That weird lady."

"That's my wife."

"That's your wife?"

"Yes it is."

"She said I was a pervert for my comic book."

"I heard about your comic book."

"My brother gave it to me the first day," he said.

"Your parents don't know about it, I bet."

"No way."

I glanced at his nightstand, only flowers.

"It's in my cast," he said.

"Ah-ha."

"You know what?"

"What."

"I heard the doctors talking about making me an experimental case. They want to replace me bit by bit."

"I bet they do," I said.

"Pretty soon I'm going to be like RoboCop."

"No kidding."

"No, for real they might have to replace my knee with a steel one," he said. "It's all twisted up."

"Sorry to hear that."

Nadia turned over again. I put my hand on the back of her head and smoothed her hair — the rash had spread there, too, to the backs of her ears, scaly and moist, the cracks glistening with lymph.

And she stayed sick. At home we packed, perfunctorily. The red Qantas envelopes sat in their place on the banister. But nothing changed with Nadia. She didn't get better, she didn't get worse, her fever never went below a hundred and one. I visited her before and after work all week. Her IV bag emptied and was replaced; the back of her hand around the needle was bruised dark as an Oreo. She would wake up occasionally and say hello, her voice hoarse, her palate swollen and red when I peered in, and I would say hello back, touch her face. Ted came after school and read aloud from his book, sitting with his legs crossed, his big dark head bent over the pages. Every day he bought a single orange soda in a paper cup for sixty-five cents. Nurses came by in red fur hats, sang "Jingle Bells" and "O Christmas Tree." The rash traveled over her body like a scabby raft: it left her face and traveled down her neck and back, across her stomach, drifting, and I imagined something about the size of my palm moving under her skin, some unformed thing lost, looking for a place to fasten itself. Harriet rubbed it with salves and balms till it was shiny as a playing card, but it traveled on.

On Thursday evening, with Nadia asleep, and rain nittering against the dark windows, I said, "We should call about the tickets."

"Sure," Harriet said. She was reading *Gene.*

"She shouldn't have taken this long."

"She's getting better," Harriet said. "It's taking a while, that's all."

"We could push the trip back a week."

"You don't want a week there. It's two days' travel just getting there and getting back."

"I know."

"So we'll cash in the tickets."

"Ted'll be disappointed," I said.

"And you won't?"

"Well, I will be too," I said. "But I'm worried about what he'll think."

"Well," she said, "I'm sorry. There's next year."

"I know."

"He'll understand." She wiped Nadia's lips. "It's not as if they're not refundable."

"No, I know."

"So. Maybe this spring I'll have some time," she said.

"I doubt it."

She laughed. The magazine slid off her lap. "You're so pissy."

"No I'm not."

"You are. It's not like we haven't gone anywhere together."

"I haven't been there in thirty-five years."

"So what's another year?" she said, and I didn't want to nod at the bed and say, *What if I'm like that, or what if I'm dead, or what if you decide to leave?* Things were precarious enough already.

After Harriet left that night, I read to Nadia. She was snuggled small against me, tired and weak, though she was better, a little — she hadn't opened her eyes all day, but she wasn't so hot as before. We followed the boys through the emir's palace, abandoned now a hundred years, a messy, complicated place: satin pillows had turned to powder in dusty chambers, vines spiraled down the walls. Big, unidentifiable fruit dropped rotting on the floor. Tigers roamed lax and supple down the halls, sleek and pettable, the tame descendants of the emir's old clowder. Marble statues had fallen to the stone floors, so arms and legs lay here and there, alabaster and perfectly formed. Red birds flashed across the open courtyard. *This certainly isn't Perth,* Ewing said, staring — and then, in that little blue room, my daughter shrugged against my chest, complaining, I think, and I stopped reading. I put the book down, and I imagined a long view of my city, as if from the air and slightly out to sea — a charitable view from a distance, a scene of white walls and stone bridges, wharves, alleys, my bright childhood city — and then I made it go away; I forgot about it, or resolved to do so. There would be other times.

Dustin stirred and opened his eyes and said, "Keep going."

"Later," I said.

Friday evening at home (it was raining again, and we had a fire going) Ted and I put up a Christmas tree, halfheartedly, in the corner of the living room. We got our hands pitchy, and I barked at him a few times for letting it fall over, but eventually it stayed up. Then into the basement for the ornaments — the red balls, the pink glittering acorns, the angels, the star. We were two men laboring together, and that felt good. He liked helping, and he played along, trying not to smile. I turned on the stereo: choral music, tenors in a vast stone church. I had a beer and read the paper in the living room, the tree winking gaudily in the corner. Ted brought down his gifts, three square boxes meticulously wrapped and tagged, and arranged them under the tree. It was the twentieth of December. Edith wouldn't be back till after the new year, and messes were already beginning to gather in the corners.

Ted disappeared again and came back with a huge fold-out map of Australia — it was four feet on a side, and had an inset of New Zealand in the upper right-hand corner. I recognized it: we'd got it from the travel agent, and I had dropped it in the bathtub, so it was wrinkled and crispy. "Going somewhere?" I asked.

Ted opened a blue spiral notebook. "Nope."

I got down on my knees beside him, conscious of my beery breath, my adult bulk. "What's up?" I said.

"I'm writing a sequel to that book." He smoothed the map with his palms. "I've got a good plot."

"What's that?"

"I think I'm going to have them get kidnaped," he said. "It's going to be an Australian adventure."

"You liked the book?"

"I thought the ending was pretty stupid."

With my finger, I traced the border of New South Wales: desert, mountains. "I've forgotten what happens at the end."

"It was stupid. They went home and nobody'd noticed they were gone."

"Oh, yeah," I said.

"And they'd been gone, like, a year or something."

"I remember. That *was* stupid."

"So I'm going to write a sequel."

"You'd better have a good ending."

"I haven't figured that out yet," he said. "I'm still fixing their route. I know how I'm going to start, though."

"How?"

"Well, I think they're going to get kidnaped by a guy who needs little kids for a burglary because they can fit through some bars that he can't fit through."

"Not bad."

"And they're going to go rob this museum for him, except they take something they're not supposed to take, and then they get in trouble for some reason. After that I don't know."

"Sounds better than the original." I leaned into him, bumping him with my shoulder. "Will I get to read it?"

"I guess so."

"Good." I said, "I hope you're not mad about not going this year."

"No, I'm not mad. I'm disappointed." He wouldn't look at me. "I wanted to do some research."

"Sure."

"Also, I wanted *you* to go," he said.

"I know you did."

"I think you would've had a really great time."

"Well, I do too," I said.

"I think it'd have been good for Mom."

"Probably."

"She's been pretty cranky lately."

"She's got a tough job," I said.

"I think she needs a vacation."

"Maybe she does."

"You should take her somewhere. Take her to Idaho or something. Someplace weird."

"Idaho."

"I don't know. Somewhere."

"I've been cranky, too, though," I said. "I don't know if she'd want to go with me."

"Maybe not."

I got back up on the sofa and finished my beer. "I liked how you came and read to your sister," I said. "Her fever's getting better."

"That Dustin kid gives me the creeps," he said. "He was like making faces at me the whole time."

"You see his leg?"

"Yeah. Totally gross. Also he kept trying to interrupt me."

"He's probably pretty bored."

"No excuse to be rude," Ted said. He laughed. "Mom wants to throw him out the window."

"I know."

"Aaaaah!" He splatted himself comically on the carpet. "I'm dayuhd," he said.

Saturday, when the boys meet the emir, he is locked in a bottle. Nadia, who seems better still, brushes my chin with her hand. She is beginning to see things clearly again, and she's staring: at my pores, my stubble, the pointy end of my nose. She says, Your nose is all *sharp. Ssh ssh*, I say, putting her hand back down. *Listen*: Lionel turns the bottle this way and that, holds it up to the torch, aloft by his shoulder, a rag torch burning in this dark, wet room. A man sits inside the bottle, shrunken and asleep, in white robes, with a white headdress; he is curled around something secret, something shining that he holds at the center of his belly, even in sleep. And the boys think, What spells do they know? What words do they know to set him free? They rub the bottle, but nothing happens. Dustin leans on his elbow and watches us. *Spells*, Lionel says, *are usually quite complicated, according to what I've read.* Can the emir grant wishes? Can he tell them the safe way home? They set the bottle carefully on the ground, consider stomping it, decide not to, pick it up again, and see the emir awake and gazing at them, serene, distant, his dark eyes tiny but triumphant. Ted is writing in the corner, smiling to himself, his paper cup beside him on the table. Nadia is staring at her fingers, entranced, as if they're about to speak.

When the fever finally relented three days later — gone without reason, without explanation, her illness never having been precisely diagnosed, her drugs never having fully taken hold — we brought her home. I carried her upstairs to bed, where she poked curiously at the dark spot on the back of her hand as if it were a button, as if a slot would slide open in her chest; for a few minutes she sat and looked out her window at the back yard, her familiar view. Then she slept and slept, still weak, still tired. What exactly had she had? A stubborn strep, Harriet decided, though it hadn't acted like strep. It hadn't acted like anything.

In bed that night — our plane had gone off in the afternoon, and we'd have been on it, only halfway to Guam — with Harriet beside me, I said, "Ted thinks we should take a vacation. You and me, I mean."

She said nothing. The dark multiplied around us, came in waves, a cloudy night, orange through the skylight.

I said, "He said we should go to Idaho."

"No thanks."

"No, I think he was kidding. But," I said, "sounds nice. Be sort of nice to each other for a while?"

"I think I'm fairly nice," she said.

"Well," I said. "Sometimes."

"And then there's you, Mister Distant, Mister Nowhere." She snorted. "Mister Say Nothing."

"That's what I mean," I said. "I don't know why you say things like that."

"Well, no — you, Alvin, you think I'm an idiot, don't you?" She propped herself up on an elbow and poked me. "You think I don't know what you're thinking all the time, as if I don't know what goes on with you, with your little fancy ideas about me and having Ted all to yourself, this little thing where you're off in your own little fucking world with Ted and Nadia and you're pretending I don't even exist, and you just don't give a shit about whether I want to have any *part* of it, and you're always avoiding me because you think I'll bite your head off, and you know *what,* Alvin?" She began to cry. "I think they're afraid of me *too* now, they think I'm some sort of *monster* because of the way you *avoid* me so much." She said, "Oh, *shit,*" and wiped her eyes and flung herself back on the bed. "Fucking telling your own kids all these lies about me."

"I don't tell them lies," I said. "I don't know what you're talking about."

"You may as well, the way you act around me."

"I think sometimes you do scare them," I said. "You do yell a lot."

"Oh, *shit,* Alvin. No more than you do."

"Maybe not," I said. "But I don't scare them."

"Shit, you do too," she said. "Ted's scared to death of you. He cringes when you walk upstairs."

"Oh, for chrissake, Harriet, he does not."

"He does too! You should *see* him when you're not around! He's just like this normal *kid* who has this normal sort of life and then you come around and he's all *serious* again, like he's in training or something for the fucking Master Class."

"He likes it."

"He only likes it because you do. It's nothing he'd like on his own. Everything else is some little fantasy you've invented."

"Well," I said. I thought of his dazed eyes, his persistence. "Maybe."

"It's true."

"He asks me to do it with him, though," I said. "I'm supposed to say No, you can't ask me these things? I can't do that."

"Just don't be so fucking *promotional* about it all the time. It's like you're selling chocolate bars or something." She mimicked me: "Hey, Ted, wanna do some chromosomes?"

I said nothing. What could I say to that? We stared through the skylight together for a long time, silent. No wind tonight, no rain.

"We'll go next year," she said, finally. And, to my surprise, she huddled against me, her breathing deep and even, directly into my ear, as if she were imparting secrets without words, without secrecy.

It was decided we would send Ted to San Diego to see my mother. I told him the next morning when he was unpacking — he had quietly refused to unpack before our plane took off, and now, this morning, he was unzipping his bags, settling his clothes carefully back in their drawers. "A week in San Diego," I said. "A consolation prize."

"When would I leave?"

"You could leave right after Christmas, if you wanted." I sat at his desk. "Next weekend."

Ted stopped unpacking.

"I know it's not the same," I said. I put my hand on his notebook and opened it.

Ted put his suitcase back on the bed, began packing again.

"Your grandmother'd really like to see you," I said.

"That'd be fun," Ted said, quietly, taking a handful of socks.

I glanced down and read Ted's first precise sentence: *My father and I live in Perth in a tiny white house with a wall around the garden,* it read; and a little bloom of secretive joy burst open in my heart.

Nadia and I finished the book that week. She was sitting up, her eyes bright, her hair orderly, her nightgown buttoned around her neck. She could enjoy it now: Dad reading to her, soup in bed, all the television she wanted, Christmas almost here. The boys found the magic words written on the wall, and the emir exploded out of his bottle, and he showed them how to follow the orange vines toward the exit, he gave them gold coins in leather bags for saving him. *Are they rich?* she asked, and I said, *You bet they're rich.* They took a spice ship home, and the captain let them jump into the holds, where cloves were piled like tiny teeth, and cinnamon bark curled like letters, and one morning, still far out at sea, they could see Perth, and I imagined they recognized the Normandy Hotel, towering on the shore. So let's say Harriet and I make it: let's say I apologize, and she apologizes, and let's say we make it with each other in whatever final way people do, settling on certain things. Let's say this happens. If that happens, then I'm certain we'll eventually go to Perth, and we'll be careful — we won't swim after eating, and we'll heed the shark warnings, beware the traffic, avoid the bad parts of the city. The Normandy will stand shining in the holiday sun — there'll be a crowded pool and thin white towels, but the kids'll love it, the free soap, the other children, strange, accented, the little attractions and peeks they get around corners, and years later they'll both remember happily that hotel, running down the carpeted halls, the leathery tropical trees reaching to our balcony, the bellhops wheeling breakfast to the door, the way the hotel stood out against the water, strong, precise, unchanging, the solid keeper of my precious cargo, these two damaged packages of my detailed dreams.

# In Spain, One Thousand and Three

MARTIN TUTTLEMAN, alone in his dark office, sat with his feet on his glass desk and a phone in the crook of his neck. "Almost there," he said.

On his computer screen — the only bright thing in the office — a small brown monkey went floating over a brick wall, gracefully, like a balloon. Martin watched it with detached affection, the way he might have watched a neighbor's child, and plucked the phone off his shoulder.

"So it's the first left after the turtle farm," he said.

"Bull," said the boy.

"No, it is," Martin said gently. "You're on the *second* level, okay, and you turn *left* after the turtle farm, and then you grab the axe and you can go over the wall." Martin heard a dishwasher in the boy's house — something throaty and mechanical, at any rate — and a distant door closing. It was midafternoon, Friday.

"I've got a girlfriend," said the boy, quietly.

"Yeah?"

"Yeah. She's a good lay."

Martin said, "How old are you?"

"Eleven."

"Oh my God."

"Fuck you," said the boy, and hung up.

Martin clicked the line closed. Immediately his telephone began beeping again, and he watched it suspiciously until it stopped. From far down the hall he could hear other phones beeping, and a low genial burble, as though a dozen televisions were playing. He'd never had this sort of thing happen before — he'd been answering phones for almost five months — and there was a handbook they'd given him, "Harassment and Sexual Issues," but he didn't know where it was. He'd probably thrown it away. He'd certainly never read it.

His telephone beeped again, and he picked it up, cautiously, but it was another kid, a girl this time, asking another question: How do I get out of the Zone of Silence? "Get the helmet and go up the spiral staircase," he said. "But you need two globes to get through the hall."

"Goddamn," said the girl.

This is what he did all day, and at times it became relentless. After work his eyeballs burned beneath their lids. But he liked his job — the conspiratorial atmosphere, for one thing, getting forty thousand dollars a year to give away secrets, money he'd never expected. He was only twenty-five years old, and no one his age made this sort of money — no one he knew, anyway — and he'd had to quit his designing job upstairs because his wife, Evelyn, had become sick and then, horribly, had died — twenty-four and dead of bone cancer, wasting away over the course of eleven months. After nine weeks away from work he'd found himself transferred downstairs, to Customer Service — not a permanent move, supposedly, though no one knew when he'd be sent back upstairs. They'd given his job to some replacement who'd unexpectedly done well, and as a result they were in this *bind*, they couldn't knock *that* guy out, and they couldn't give Martin another job — the only other job up there was in Personnel, and that wouldn't do; he'd just have to wait until something in Design opened up. Of course they said they were sorry to do it, to demote him this way, but Martin didn't think anybody sounded particularly sorry. Now when he guided kids around the games he found little traps he'd invented himself: an island that sailed away from shore, a plane that disappeared off the top of the screen, never to return. It was odd, encountering these things again, like finding notes he'd left to himself, and he was often surprised at his old ingenuity, as though his mind had worked better upstairs in the low-ceilinged crucible of late nights and absolute deadlines. People were more relaxed down here in Service, but in most important ways he was unhappy. Much of this had to do with Evelyn, whom he missed terribly.

The Ignis building was in downtown Seattle, a big glassy box on the waterfront. When the blinds were up in his office Martin could see the jagged white Olympics and the smooth gray carpet of the Sound, but he usually worked with the blinds down, the Ignis giving its pale, unearthly light to the walls. People made fun of him for this: *You'll ruin your eyes,* they said, and he played along, he squinted and fumbled for his coffee. "You in there, Mr. Caveman?" Lily Brendan would say, bumping her round hips against his doorjamb. "You're *hiding* from us in here," she'd say.

"Oh, not from you," he'd answer. "Never from you."

She'd click her tongue. "*Martin,*" she'd say, peering in. There's a time and place for *this* sort of darkness, she meant. She'd shake her head, and Martin would watch her walk away down the hall, her body compact and strong. She was living with Jack Halloran, his boss, but recently Martin had imagined her big hips much too often, what they'd be like, and her pudgy feet in the air, and her face, how it might become contorted during sex, strained and dramatic. He'd been having these kinds of thoughts dozens of times a day since Evelyn died, and not only about Lily Brendan, either, but all sorts of women — just about every woman he saw, in fact. Women in the crosswalk, in the building lobby, gripped him, held his attention too long; he watched hips and legs climb the carpeted stairs ahead of him, and ankles with their tapering Achilles' blades, and hundreds of little conical breasts facing him in the elevators, and he felt a loathing for himself, and was saddened, too, by his faithlessness. He told himself it was normal, that it could be seen as some sort of compensatory action for three years of monogamy — though in college he'd thought about women this way, too, so maybe that wasn't quite right. In any case, it was getting out of hand. The other day he'd found himself aroused by the bouncing breasts of Lakoor the Avenger in her skin-tight leotard, three inches high on the screen. She'd held her narrow hands in front of her as though about to catch a basketball, and Martin had looked guiltily around his empty office before taking the cartridge out.

\*　　\*　　\*

An hour later the boy called back. "It's not working," he said.

"What's not working?"

"He still can't get over the wall."

"Then you've got a defective cartridge."

"It isn't working."

"No, I think it is," Martin said. "I think it's working just fine, and you're not telling me the truth."

After a moment, the boy, defeated, said, "Yeah, it's working."

"Ha," Martin said, slamming down the phone. "You little shit-head."

At home Martin had a glass of wine and opened the balcony door. He looked out over Lake Washington, at the white boats and the gray, populated hills. Alone now in the apartment he felt its size and ostentation, the white walls that met perfectly with the white baseboards, the unsettling sense of too much room. The refrigerator still clinked with Evelyn's tall colorful jars: her fancy jams, her French sauces and spreads. All of these were rotten now, he suspected, but he hadn't the heart to get rid of them. He had resolved to move, too, but that hadn't happened either. They'd often talked about buying a house but had never got around to it, and now when he was especially sad he imagined what their house might have looked like: the shrubs in the yard, the iron fence, the brick path, the rooms beyond rooms unseen. In his sadness he would wander through this nonexistent house and see her everywhere: fixing dinner, bending to pet the cat, standing at the bathroom sink to brush her hair. Often this just saddened him further, the thought that there was, somewhere in the world, the house they would have lived in. The apartment, of course, was not the same at all.

He brought the telephone to the balcony, leaned on the railing, and called his mother across town. "So I've got this extra opera ticket tonight," he said when she picked up. "I could use some company."

His mother, distracted, said, "Oh, you."

"Yeah. It's me."

"It's *Tycho,* isn't it. I hear it's terrible."

"Who said that?"

"Oh, everybody. I don't think I'm interested."

He shifted the phone from one ear to the other. "So maybe I could come over for dinner?"

"Well, all right." She cleared her throat. "That's good, Martin. We haven't seen enough of you. It's beginning to be time."

"I guess it is." He spat experimentally over the railing. The late summer lake reached out in front of him, holding the sky.

Martin's mother, who taught religion at the university, kept college girls as boarders in her big timbered house. She felt safer with them there, she said, and she liked the company. There'd been dozens over the years — all vegetarians and all women, and sometimes three or four at once. These women had tramped up and down the dark stairs, swept the yellow cherry leaves off the deck in back, hung their crumpled nylons in the shower, and before he met Evelyn — back when he'd slept with every woman he could — Martin had entertained fantasies of creeping into these women's bedrooms and hiding in their closets, he'd imagined them peeling their stockings from their legs, their various breasts falling into view. He'd had a house key; he could have managed it.

But these days Maria Relzina was his mother's only boarder, an Oregon girl who was studying biology. Maria had lived with his mother for years, and the two had become friends; they went on vacations together, went shopping for antiques in the Skagit Valley. It made Martin a little uneasy, as though his mother had adopted Maria because of some insufficiency on his part — not that he wouldn't admit to a number of insufficiencies: he would, if anyone ever asked. He wasn't the best son in the world. But something about the arrangement felt disloyal.

Now Maria stood on the porch in a long white dress, sweeping dust into the yard. A sprinkler hissed, spraying the sidewalk.

"Hello," he said. He waggled his tie at her.

"Martin. Been a long time." Her white dress glowed prettily in the dusk. She leaned against the broom. "You look okay for once."

"Thanks. Nice dress."

"Oh, ha!" Maria twisted her hips. "Keeps off the bugs." Her neck was slender, and her black hair hung over her shoulders. Beneath her dress her breasts were small, like eggs bundled in cotton. She was wearing sandals, and her feet were wide and dusty. Martin watched the hem settle around her calves. She saw him watching.

"See something?"

"I think so," he said.

"You think so?"

"I've always thought so," he said. Of course this wasn't true; he'd hardly noticed her before Evelyn died. But here she was, frank, pretty, with her long smooth calves, her heavy eyebrows, and suddenly, before he could stop himself, he thought of her running before him up a flight of stairs, and then he imagined her asleep beside him, her hair on the pillow. He winced, embarrassed, and turned away.

"You," she said, "are a flirt."

"Sorry."

"Oh, hoof, don't apologize." She leaned the broom against the railing, took his hand, and led him quickly into the house, back through the long dark hallway to the kitchen. Her hand, plump and firm as a pear, rested easily in his, and when they reached the kitchen she said, "Guess who's here."

His mother sat at the kitchen table, doing a crossword. "Oh, it's the man himself," she said, rising, a little gray gnome, to embrace him. Her white hair sat piled on her head, and she smelled damp and leafy, like the garden. "I've ordered a pizza for us, hope you don't mind. I'm not up to the cooking thing."

"That's all right."

Maria ducked out of the kitchen and ran outside, laughing.

His mother looked darkly at him. "You see that? She's been in a strange mood lately."

Before he could stop himself, he asked, "Boyfriend troubles?"

"Maria?" She pursed her lips and put her finger to them. "No, I don't think so. She used to date this awful boy named Laramie who was a terrible cold fish, but he was a short-timer. I don't think that's what's on her mind." She opened the refrigerator and handed Martin a bottle of beer. "Don't *you* start thinking about it. She's not your style."

"I don't know what you mean."

"Oh, *yes* you do, Martin, that playboy thing you used to do. I'll kill you if you lay a *finger* on her."

After a moment he said, uneasily, "I don't do that sort of thing anymore."

"Well, she was really an innocent when she came to live with me, you know; knew absolutely nothing at all about the world. But now she's really very *skeptical* — in a good way, I mean. I think she's becoming a Buddhist."

"She's from Eugene."

"Oh, don't laugh, Martin, that's nasty. And it's the only sensible religion there is. The fundamental principle of the world is its illusory nature." She peered into the depths of the refrigerator, pushed aside a wrapped sandwich, and took out a beer for herself, a tall dark bottle. "Everything that exists comes from the mind. And yet the world is holy, and God lives in all things. It's wonderful. Even if it's not true, it should be."

He shrugged. What could be said? There weren't any words; he'd stopped trying to find them a while ago. People took this silence as sadness, and that was part of it. But more than anything he'd simply stopped trying to figure things out. He was exhausted. Abruptly he said, "You know, I don't have anything to say anymore."

His mother, holding the bottle opener, eyed him as though he were a misspelled sign. "Yes?"

"I mean I don't *talk* anymore, hardly, except at work. I don't even *think* about anything anymore." He paused. "I don't know if you know what I mean."

"I do." She smiled and pushed her glasses up her nose. "It's normal."

"People keep telling me that."

"It's true. It's to be expected."

"I guess so," he said. Of course there was more, but he couldn't talk about sex with his mother. He never had, not really.

When the pizza arrived, the boy in his plastic hat lingered on the front porch, smiling at Maria. She patted the flat pockets of her dress for money, then leaned the broom against her shoulder, cradling it. Martin watched her through the porch windows, and he thought, as he did every day, many times a day, of Evelyn, her high bed and its aluminum rails, and he felt again the pit that had opened in him, perhaps forever. It was nothing like he'd imagined it would be, in the weeks when they knew she was dying. He'd expected sorrow, naturally, and missing her, but he hadn't anticipated this gigantic hole. Sometimes the entire thing was, in its way, embarrassing, as any public infirmity might have been, obliging people to be sympathetic and understanding, though he felt he didn't deserve any sympathy.

Maria walked quickly past him in the hall as she headed for the kitchen, holding the pizza box above her head. "Beep-beep," she said, and he watched her disappear around the corner, her elbows angular, her long neck bending gracefully. Again he imagined her rolling in bed beside him, not a sordid image, he knew, but it saddened him anyway, because this was how he had thought of Evelyn in their days together, and he turned back to the table, his hands unsteady with shame and lust.

But he did know bodies — or at least he'd had more sex than anyone he knew. He was thirteen when he seduced a neighbor, Constance Tiptin, on the carpet, when his mother was out of town. It was not Constance's first time, and she'd watched him through narrowed eyes while he worked, briefly, above her. Constance lasted a few months, then came Julie with the black bangs, and the damp folds of her blouse under his hands, and then in high school he'd had sex with one girl after another, a few dozen in all, probably, though he'd never bothered to count. In college he'd averaged three or four a month, women from the vast university population whom he rarely saw again. He was handsome, they said, and he supposed he was charming. He knew he was a good talker, and he was drawn to the variety of bodies, the hundred ways a breast could lift and settle, the different ways women laughed and became nervous or forthright when they took off their clothes and tossed them away, or draped them carefully over the back of his chair, with the streetlight playing over their skin. He acquired a reputation for being something of a libertine, and he deserved it, though he didn't care.

He met Evelyn in one of his English classes. She sat near the door and said almost nothing, but she was pretty — dark eyes — and during class she moved her head slowly back and forth, as if hearing music. One day, after class, with the other students trailing away like refugees, he spoke to her, invited her to a movie. She shrugged, accepted, and after the movie she invited him back to her apartment, where, hefting a box off the sofa, she told him to sit down. She put on a recording of Casals, suites for cello unaccompanied. "Listen to this," she said. She pushed her hair behind her ears.

Though he knew nothing about music, Martin suspected he was being seduced, and certainly he would go along. But to his surprise he liked the creaking and groaning of the cello, like a ship tossing at sea. Evelyn didn't sit next to him; she leaned against one end of the sofa, watching his face. She hummed, her big goofy teeth resting on her bottom lip, and Martin wanted her: her thighs in her jeans, her solid upper arms heavy in her green sweater. The cello creaked on, dust popping in the seams of vinyl. She held her finger up as the music climbed, joyfully; put her palm down and looked sad as the music descended and became somber again, chestnut-dark, confined. "All right," she said, when the record ended. "You can go now."

"Go?"

"Please go," she said. And he went, puzzled. This rarely happened, and he wondered, briefly, what he'd done wrong, and promptly forgot about it. But that weekend she called and asked him to the movies, and the marquee lights on her face reminded him of those other women's bodies lit through his window. Over coffee that night she pushed up the sleeves of her sweater. Her hands were heavy and strong. "I *play* the cello, as a matter of fact," she said, and back in her apartment she lifted the thing from its black case. It was brown and sculpted like a body, but light, and she spun it deftly on its stand and then sat with it between her knees. "What to play?" she said, staring over his head.

"Whatever. I'd like to hear anything you've got."

"I'm trying to impress you. But I don't think you're easily impressed."

"I'm already impressed."

"No, I asked around about you," she said, squinting at him. "I know what you do."

"And here I am."

"You've got a reputation," she said, sternly. "You think that's how you're supposed to behave? Because it's not. You're supposed to stick with one woman."

He said nothing. He leaned forward and touched her knee.

"I shall play *The Flight of the Bumblebee*," she said, shifting away. But she was smiling. "Transposed for cello unaccompanied."

"Great," he said, idiotically.

All at once she began to bow with great vigor, ignoring him. He smiled uncomfortably and tried to nod with the music, but it was much too fast. He fell into a sort of trance, watching her. Her fingers flashed on the neck of the cello, she gritted her teeth, her hair hung over her eyes. For a minute she was magnificently ugly, tense and contorted. When they moved in together after college he remembered this night, and it wasn't so much that he'd fallen in love with her music or her passion as with her scolding: she sneered the first time they climbed into bed together, which unsettled him. And as they got to know each other in the weeks after this night she made fun of him for having the reputation he had, and quickly he became ashamed of it. "I bet you've slept with *her*," she'd say, pointing across the street as they walked through the terraced campus to one of her concerts. "*She* looks like your type."

"They were all my type," he'd say.

After graduation they shopped for pots, and mingled their books, and in this new life of his he felt calmer, more adult. He studied her music, learning slowly its strange, bright-faceted landscape, and though he still loved sex he found he thought only of her body: its dips and hollows, her solid, round rump, her underarm hair swishing against his fingers. For three good years she filled his hands; but now he had begun imagining the bodies of his mother's boarders again, and Lily Brendan's body, and his own body had begun betraying him, wanting the surfaces of things, the pale appearances. Of course his mother was right: paradise was the absence of desire, and hell — or this particular version of hell — was desire everlasting.

The boy called first thing Monday morning. "I got to level four and I'm stuck," he said.

"You again. You should be in school."

"I'm sick. I have the flu."

"You don't sound sick."

"I am, though."

Martin tipped back in his chair and turned on the Ignis. From far away down the hall he heard someone laughing. He keyed himself into the fourth level. "What's your name?" Martin asked.

"Oscar."

"All right, Oscar. You've got to promise not to lie to me."

"I didn't lie to you."

"Sure you did." He thought of giving him false hints — he had done this before to particularly awful children — but it had got him in trouble with Halloran, his boss, and he hesitated to do it again.

"No I didn't."

"There's a yellow blimp that flies over on level four," said Martin, quietly. "It's got an extra life in it. Throw a Barterball at it."

Oscar breathed.

"Also, try to fool around with the porcupines for a while and see what happens."

"What happens?"

"Something good."

"You won't tell me what happens?"

"No," Martin said.

"Hey," Oscar said, calmly, "that's your job. You *have* to tell me."

"I don't have to tell you anything," he said, nastily. "It's in my contract. I don't have to give secrets to liars."

"I didn't lie to you, I just couldn't figure it out."

"I doubt that."

"I'm sick," Oscar said. "My brain's not working right."

"No kidding."

"Oh, man," Oscar said.

Martin waited. The line hummed. "What," he said, finally.

"Man, you should have seen it." The boy's voice was thick and conspiratorial. "We were all like going at it? And she was all like *juicy.*"

"Oh, Jesus," Martin said, and hung up. He looked uneasily at the phone. At once it rang, and he unplugged it from the wall. He patted down his hair with the palm of one hand. He'd had weirdos before, but they'd been adults.

He was bending forward to plug in the telephone again when Jack Halloran knocked on the doorjamb. "Martin," he said. "Talk to you for a minute?"

"Sure."

He came in and shut the door, and suddenly the office grew dark. Halloran went to the window and pulled up the blinds. It was a sunny day, and a freighter sat anchored in the harbor. Lean and bearded, dressed in a flannel shirt, his dark eyes glistening, Halloran turned to Martin and said, "You don't look too good."

Martin blinked in the bright light. "This kid keeps calling me. Nasty one."

"What's he doing?"

"Telling me he's had sex with his girlfriend."

"What's he, thirteen?"

"Eleven." Martin turned off his desk lamp.

"Yeah, I've had those." Halloran touched his beard, smoothed it with his hand. "What'd you say to him?"

"Hung up on him."

"That's what I do. The fuckheads." Halloran turned and looked out the window at the view. He sighed, his thin shoulders rising, falling, and said, "So listen, I was talking to Ed Miles up in Design."

"Yeah?"

"He says there's a spot open for you, if you want it, at the end of the month. Some guy's leaving."

"Did he say who?"

"I wrote it down."

Martin nodded. He thought, without much fondness, of the cluttered, flashing offices. Ed Miles was an asshole; he'd called Martin Tie-Boy because he'd worn a tie to work, and though eventually he stopped wearing it, the name had stuck, becoming, eventually, Teebo, then T-Bone. The hours were longer and harder, and the whole fourth floor smelled bitter, having absorbed the resinous hormones of thirty pale young men. And the games were horrible, a series of tortures — snakes, devils, death, no escape — and your players were born over and over into the same terrible worlds, which got dispiriting after a while. The money was better, though.

"I know this job is kind of beneath you in a lot of ways." Halloran turned to face him. "I wouldn't take it badly if you went back upstairs. I know that's what you came here for."

"Thanks." Martin shrugged. "I might. I sort of like it here."

"Do you mind if I ask you something?"

"What."

"I'm sort of wondering if you're seeing anyone these days."

"Seeing anyone?"

"Like dating," Halloran said.

"Me? No." He turned off the computer and looked at the ceiling, the porous tiles. "Not dating."

"I was just wondering, sort of on a personal level," Halloran said. "But I guess not."

"No."

"Lily and I were talking." Halloran picked at one of his fingernails. "It was kind of a fight. Not about you, I mean. About us."

"Yeah?"

"Yeah. She's bored with me, I think. I mean, she won't come out and say it. But that's the impression. She's bored with me."

"Well."

"So," Halloran said, "I was wondering if you knew anything about that sort of thing. Like keeping a woman's interest."

"Oh," he said, "I don't know. Give her a change. Buy a new jacket or something."

Halloran peered at him. "You must miss her," he said, suddenly. "You never talk about it with anybody around here."

After a moment Martin said, "It's tough to talk about."

"Yeah. My dad died a couple years ago, I know what it's like, I guess. More or less."

"Sure." Martin looked down at his hands and saw they were balled into fists. He regarded them curiously, then relaxed them, one finger at a time. His palms were blotched with pink.

"I could set you up with someone if you want."

"No." He examined his desk. "No, thanks."

"Lily and I were just wondering."

"I think it's a little soon."

"I guess you stop thinking about it for a while. More important stuff to think about."

"Something like that," said Martin. But this was exactly the way his body was betraying him. *The body's just a dirty jar,* his mother would say, *just a dirty jar for the soul.* In fact he'd wanted Evelyn's body even on her worst days, not exactly against doctor's orders but skirting them. They'd gone slowly because she was often dry and uncomfortable, and she'd had to lie still, with her eyes closed: finding the pleasure of sex was difficult, a task of concentration — like following a dark shape in a dark room, she told him later. She held her head back, studying the movements they made. He'd wanted her constantly, and it embarrassed him to want her when she weighed a hundred pounds or less, when she was sick and dizzy, when her purse clicked with vials, or when he'd cut off her hair. In the end he had taken sexual interest in her hands and face: he'd put his tongue in the dry spaces between her fingers and she stirred, breathing carefully; and her forehead, which he would kiss and breathe on; and her ears, stiff and waxless. He had never stopped wanting her. And after she'd died sitting up, and he had passed through the tunnel of the next horrible week at his mother's house, in his old bedroom, in the dark, he had awakened in the morning and wanted Maria. He'd listened to Maria padding back and forth to the bathroom upstairs, and the water running in the shower, and he'd imagined the soap sliding over her belly and the wet slap of her hair. He waited for these imaginings to go away, but they had continued. And though he had done nothing yet, Martin feared, as Halloran left his office, that he soon would do something, that his body would demand its satisfaction, and that Evelyn would be gone, then, for good, the memory of her body absorbed into the feel of another woman's body, as a twin absorbs the tissues of its twin.

After work on Monday he drove to Ballard. Evelyn's parents had been in Mexico for six months, and now they wanted to see him. They met him at the door, tanned and smelling of liquor. "Well, hell, Martin," Peter said, shaking hands. He had big shoulders, rough palms, sandy hair: a Swede. "It's good to see you, buddy."

"Thanks. You too."

"Oh, Martin." Josephine was skinny and had short brown hair. She embraced him, and the big yellow beads around her neck clacked like teeth. She held Martin at arm's length. "You are so *pale*."

"Oh, I think I'm about right," he said.

Josephine laughed and then began to cry, mildly. "Martin," she said. She clawed a tear away with a brown hand. She sniffed and recovered. "Whoops. Didn't see that one coming."

Peter patted her shoulder. "It's all right."

"We were just having a drink, and I'm getting all mooshy." She sighed. "We're turning into drinkers."

"No, we're not," Peter said.

They moved into the living room: small, blue-carpeted, with

fringed lamps. "We haven't talked to your mother in ages," Josephine said. "She's all right, I hope."

"Well, you know my mother. Nothing quite gets to her. But she's fine."

"She's a strong woman," Josephine said, plopping into a chair. "I admire her for that."

Martin took a whiskey. He sat. The room reeked of booze.

"Gackie," said Peter. The dog, brown and leathery like a suitcase, trotted through the room and out again, ignoring everyone.

"The dog's the same," Martin said.

Peter rubbed his knees. "Fucking dog," he said.

"Well, I'll be teaching again soon," Josephine said, fingering her beads. "In Madrona. They couldn't get along without me."

"That's good."

"Back to the kiddies." She curled her lip.

"I've got a story for you," Martin said. He plucked at his cuff. "Had a kid tell me last week he'd had sex with his girlfriend. Eleven years old."

"Oh, no."

Peter shook his head. "This world."

"Couldn't believe it. Just came out and told me." He was angry now, for the first time. "And he keeps calling me, is the thing. He *keeps* telling me about it. That's what bugs me."

"Fucking punks."

"Yeah. I've been thinking of quitting. I hadn't thought about it seriously until now, but this kid's bugging the shit out of me. I don't know what it is. I got an offer to move back upstairs to Design, you know, so it's right there if I want it." He smiled; it was good to talk. "They're really *fucked up* upstairs, though. They don't know how to treat people, and you know, I've been thinking about why that is" — this wasn't true, he hadn't thought about it at all — "and I think it's because they don't have any women up there. It's all men."

"Oh," Josephine said.

"So they've got this sort of crotch-jockey mentality setup, you know, the code writers especially." Martin squinted, seeing it. "They've got this big scoreboard up in the lunchroom, measures lines of code, is what it does, and the guy with the most lines at the end of the week gets a bonus." He sat back and drank his whiskey, which was cool and good. "Five hundred bucks. And it *smells*. It *smells* funny up there, all those guys together. It's like a locker room. The windows don't even open. You get off the elevator and it hits you in the face. *Bam.*"

After a pause, Josephine asked, "You didn't take much time off, did you?"

"No," he said. "Two months."

"We took six months," she said. "But you know that. Ran up the credit cards."

"You guys look great."

"Thanks," Josephine said.

Then there was nothing else to say. It had come and gone, just like that.

"You were so good," Josephine said.

"Oh," he said, and there was another odd silence. He swallowed the rest of his drink.

"We have some things of yours upstairs," Josephine said.

"You do?"

"A shirt, I think," she said, waving vaguely. "Up in her room." She stood, unsteadily, and took his arm, and the two of them padded upstairs.

There, he smelled the old smells of the house: the metallic tinge of rain, somewhere, as if the roof leaked, a thick mix of onion and oil, the dusty carpet. In her bedroom things were different: the bed made, the shelves cleared. Here was their picture, his arm around her. "Yes, that," Josephine said. "That's nice, isn't it?" She was standing at the door behind him, and he could hear her breathing, and though he didn't want to Martin imagined her little breasts beneath her blouse, downturned teardrops, they'd be. Brushing past him she put a warm hand on the small of his back and went to the closet. "Your shirt," she said. The vials were gone from the dresser, the stacks of folded towels, the bowls and syringes; the telephone and television had been removed. It was a silent room now, looking out onto the wooded back yard, the fir trees. At the window he had cupped Evelyn's breasts once, from behind, and she'd twisted her hips back against him, a day when the house had owned that delicious weekday afternoon sexuality, the ease and arousal born of quiet, only the jets passing over occasionally, and the distant rainy whish of traffic.

For a while he and Josephine stood together in the room and didn't say anything. Then she opened the closet and took out his shirt, heavy white cotton, a good shirt dirtied long ago by Evelyn's vomit, washed and forgotten several times. Josephine held the shirt to him as if testing its size in a store, then she hugged him, holding his big shoulders and tucking her head beneath his chin. "Oh, Martin," she said. She was warm and soft, her hips and breasts smaller and flatter than Evelyn's, but the body was recognizable, just as easy and comfortable in his arms, and Martin lingered with her. And all at once she was rubbing against him, and he was rubbing against her, lightly, the two of them like shy dancers; there was the brush of fabric on fabric, and she swelled against him, pushing. He pushed back. And quickly they pulled apart, looking away.

Lily Brendan took him by the elbow the next morning, Tuesday. "Martin," she whispered, and dragged him aside, into the coffee room. A smell of burnt bagels hung in the air. "What exactly did you tell Jack yesterday?"

"Nothing. He said there was a job upstairs for me."

She looked to either side and behind her. "He shaved all his *body hair*," she said, urgently. Her eyes were dark with mascara, and her mouth was big and easy. "He's like a sausage. He came out of the bathroom last night and said he had a surprise. I almost burst a vessel."

"Not his head."

"No, but everything else. The beard's gone."

"Holy shit."

"It wasn't bad, though," she said, licking her lips. "I'm not complaining. He was really smooth."

"I bet." Martin cleared his throat.

"You didn't say anything to him, did you?"

"No. He asked me about Evelyn."

"Oh." Her eyebrows went up, and she nodded; this meant something, he was sure, but he couldn't tell what. "That explains it."

"He offered to set me up."

She gasped and held his arm. "I've got a friend."

"I don't think so," Martin said, blinking. But she was close to him, so close he could see the fuzz on her chin, the black crumbs of mascara in her eyelashes. He couldn't help noticing these things, and he couldn't help the way his eyes darted down to her breasts, big and solid in the flowery blouse, and to her hips, which would crash against his, muscled and demanding. He'd gone home the night before, mortified, hopelessly aroused by Josephine's satin pants, by the experienced grind of her pelvis. His voice shaking a little, he said, "You're not looking so bad yourself."

"I know I'm not," she said.

"Old Halloran doesn't know what he's got."

"Oh, I think he does." She raised her chin. "I think *you* know what he's got, too."

"I think I do."

She looked away.

"You know I have to confess," Martin whispered. "I've been thinking about it constantly. Sex, I mean."

"Oh, Martin. That's understandable."

"I mean constantly. I can't stop thinking about it. Everybody. My mother's roommate."

"Well. That's a good sign, maybe."

"It's not a sign. It's been going on ever since."

"Since when." She peered at him.

"About six months ago. A week after the funeral."

"Really?"

"Yeah, really."

"Oh, I don't think that's all that unusual," she said, but she was guarded now. "It's like people pairing off at weddings, you know. It's life affirming."

"Bullshit, life affirming. It's psychotic. I got turned on by her mother yesterday."

"Her mother?"

"Yes." He pinched his tie and sniffed. "You don't think that's unusual?"

"Well, no, it's a little unusual, I'd have to say."

"I'm not sure why I'm telling you."

"That's all right," she said.

"Listen. I don't want you to get the wrong idea. I mean, I miss her," he said, desperately. "I really do."

She smiled and patted his shoulder. "It'll be our secret."

He walked down the hall to his office. His hands were shaking, and he balled them into fists. He closed the door behind him and sat alone, in the dark, and to calm himself he pictured again, as he did almost every day, their unrealized house: the front walk, the bricks in the path, the doorknocker, the mailbox, the front door. *This is our common body,* he thought, and the idea pleased him, though he wasn't sure where it had come from. He ignored his telephone and walked through their rooms, putting things on shelves, arranging the furniture; he imagined Evelyn standing at various windows, sitting on benches, holding a pillow in her lap. It was, frustratingly, never the same house twice — the rooms shifted and grew; the house was sometimes in Laurelhurst, sometimes in Montlake — and it was a foolish, empty exercise, meaning nothing, just another fantasy. But it calmed him. After a while he stood up and lifted the blinds. It was still midmorning, and the Sound sat gray and calm under the window. A streetcar trundled down Alaskan Way, green, clanging its bells.

Halloran knocked on the door after lunch. He smiled sheepishly and touched his bald chin. "Shaved," Halloran said. His skin looked soft to the touch.

"Looks good."

"Figured it was time for a change."

"Fuckin A," Martin said. "Change is good."

Halloran looked at him closely. "You okay?"

"I'm fine."

"You sure?"

He had grown used to this sort of questioning. "Thank you for asking," he said. His telephone was beeping, and he held up a finger and answered it. Halloran disappeared.

That afternoon Oscar called. "Hey," Oscar said. "Finally."

"Oh, Jesus. You again." He'd lifted the blinds to watch the clouds roll in, so the office was bright gray. "How do you keep getting my line?"

"I call lots of times," Oscar said. "When it's not you, I hang up."

"Why the hell do you do that?"

"Because you're the one I talked to first."

Martin leaned to look down the hallway. He said, "Oscar, listen to me."

Oscar breathed.

"Oscar, you want another secret?"

"Sure."

"What level'd you get to?"

"Seven," Oscar said.

He heard a girl's voice in the background. "Who's that?" Martin asked.

"Nobody."

"*Oscar*," Martin said, ferociously. "You want a secret? Stop playing these *games*."

"Why?"

"Because they're a *big fucking waste of your time*," he said. "Throw the fucking thing out the window. You're not learning anything. You're fucking up your little *head*."

Oscar gasped.

"I can just quit," Martin said, ferociously. "Whenever I want to, buddy, I can just quit. I don't need this job. In fact, how's this? You call me one more time, I'm quitting."

"Okay," Oscar said, and hung up. Martin waited for the phone to ring again, but it didn't. One ring, he thought. He stared at the black plastic face of the telephone. Nothing happened. Outside, it began to rain. Pigeons spun chaotically in the sky.

In their years together, when he hummed her songs — and he often found himself humming idly in front of the Ignis screen, say, or in the middle of a design meeting — Martin could pretend he was inside his wife's head, which he imagined as a big ornate room filled with a series of melodies that repeated, flashing gently, maybe, like Christmas lights. He studied her, meaning he studied her music: when he was alone in the apartment he played her LPs, sitting on the sofa with the cardboard record sleeve in his lap, and he heard, occasionally, the click of a bow against a music stand or the shuffle of someone's shoes, and he liked these moments especially — the whole fancy enterprise seemed fallible somehow, and he suspected that when Evelyn's musician friends talked about the old days, and about their nostalgia for vinyl records, they were in fact nostalgic for an age when things seemed more achievable, when music was more of a human endeavor, not polished and electronic but warm and liquid, the black record revolving like a puddle of oil.

And Evelyn still played the cello, though not as much as before. She'd become a teacher and was usually worn out from work, but every so often she invited her music-teacher friends to the apartment. These women set their violin cases on the dining room table, as if setting down platters of delicate food; and after drinks, when the dinner was cooking, they'd snap open the cases. Martin liked this moment: their faces became serious, as if they were admitting they could never be perfect, that they would always be slow or clumsy, and he loved their rueful look, as if they were bringers of bad news. They would put down their wine and play, their chins tucked into their instruments. "Shit," they'd say occasionally. "Goddamn it." To Martin the music sounded seamless, but he liked to hear them swearing, well-dressed women holding their polished instruments in his big apartment. It felt like real life.

During these good years he felt he'd conquered himself. He'd considered the patterns of his life, which had been lascivious, and changed them. And Evelyn was understanding, if only because she'd done some of the same things herself. She'd slept with men whose names she'd hardly known, and she described how she would seduce a man, and to Martin's surprise, this aroused him; he liked to imagine his plump Evelyn calculating and considering frankly the aims of her body. She still looked at men, she said, still wondered what it'd be like sleeping with the principal, the bus drivers, and she'd elaborate for him the fantasies she had — their slack middle-aged bodies, their sudden hopefulness in her arms, the way their breath came in puffs, their sweet inept bodily release. Daily in the kitchen, in the steaming car parked beneath the building, leaning on the midnight balcony, she and Martin fitted themselves together, and he found he was still aroused by the sense of abandon that came with sex, with all pretenses dropped, this and only this the real reason for everything. So they were good in bed, but naturally there was more to it than that. She bought clay pots and started a garden on the balcony. He built bookshelves for her in the parking lot and hustled them upstairs on his shoulders. She turned to him in sleep, the apartment dark and ticking, creaking around them; in the dark her face would be slack and dumb, and, happily, he would watch the headlights pour over the ceiling and down the white walls.

This faith in her, this conversion, had been genuine, and he was proud of those days, those two good years. But during their third winter she started getting tired, and at the same time she was unable to sleep well, sitting up in bed: *I feel funny,* she said. Her eyes grew thin gray bags, like hammocks. On a rainy day they went to see *Don Giovanni* (they were her tickets), though she said she felt dizzy, unearthly. In their loge seats he held her hand, mildly concerned, stroking the wide strong bones of her wrist. The strings sank away at the end of the overture, and Leporello sang, roguish and importunate: *Madamina; il catalog e questo.* I've compiled a little list, he sang, of the Don's conquests. The Italian hills rolled away from him in the distance; there were colonnades and, in the valley below, red-tiled roofs. Leporello held the paper for inspection, propped his glasses on his nose. *In Italia sei cento e quaranto; cento in Francia, in Turchia novantuna; ma in Ispagna, son gia mille e tre. Mille e tre.* That profligacy, a thousand and three in Spain alone! Washerwomen, duchesses, the elderly, the infirm, the virginal. "Ah-ha," Martin said, and tapped her knee. "See? It's not so unusual."

"Don't start," she said.

"The don's my kind of guy," he said. She swallowed, uneasily.

It wasn't the next morning, or the one after that, but that weekend when she went to the doctor, and it started: the speculation, the mystery, the organic food, the worry that toxins were everywhere — that they were the real purpose of the world, the world's revenge, killing those who had killed it. Now more than ever he regretted his past, and he wondered, irrationally, whether he had pushed her over the edge by mentioning it again, resurrecting his old lecherous self for her to consider; but he knew this was ridiculous. First surgery, then chemicals; nothing worked. Like something left outside in summer, she became more fragile, more brittle. Her bodily weakness compelled him as nothing had compelled him before, as did the desperation with which she looked at him, the envy she must have felt for *his* body, sound and solid. He continued to imagine only her — first as she used to be, round and full and tight; and as she grew sicker, he accommodated himself to her new body, to its sags and fragilities. He couldn't conceive of his old sexual liberties. His former self, he thought, had been finally abolished, and in a way he was right, because until she died he wanted no one else. But it was small consolation, and now he was right back where he'd begun.

In a desperate mood he left work and took the crowded bus home, he folded his Goretex lunch bag and put it carefully in the cupboard among the soup cans and boxes of tea, he opened a bottle of wine and had a glass and another glass; he had begun his third when the front door buzzer rang. It was Maria. "Martin," she said, dryly, through the speaker.

"I think you've got the wrong apartment."

"Very funny."

He buzzed her in. He stood at the top of the stairs and watched her come up, her black hair in its yellow band, her blue dress soft on her shoulders. "You look wonderful," he said.

She passed into the apartment, scowling. "You're making your mother feel terrible, you know."

"I was kidding about the boyfriend thing."

"Well, don't kid. She doesn't know what to think. *I* don't know what to think. Obviously you're not in love with me but then you make these bizarre comments."

"Sorry about that."

"I don't think you should be living over here all by yourself, either, Martin, it's not doing you any good. You should be with us."

"No thanks." He raised his arms, indicating the empty expanse of the place. "I like being alone."

"I think this *apartment* is getting to you, too. It's a *bachelor* pad, is what it is. That's why you're doing these things." She went to the refrigerator. "Gah," she said, bending, holding her breath. She began stacking bottles on the counter. "You know you're growing thallophytes in here."

"Don't do that."

"This is disgusting." She examined a jar of chutney.

"That's Evelyn's."

"It's totally moldy."

"I know."

She put the jar on the counter. He looked at it, balefully, and sighed. "I'm going to take a shower," he said.

"Stay right here." She got a bottle of Windex and a sponge from beneath the sink. "You and I need to talk." He watched her long arm wiping.

"What about."

"Well, Josephine called today. She said you weren't quite yourself." Her voice was contained in the refrigerator.

"Oh boy."

"That poor old lady. She was drunk."

"She drinks a lot these days."

"Well, she said you made a *pass* at her. I couldn't imagine your doing that, so I said, What are you talking about? And she gave me the whole story." Maria sighed. "Tell me it isn't true."

"It's true."

She tossed a piece of cheese into the garbage. "Well, that's pretty sick, I've got to be honest. For both of you."

"Yeah."

"And then *Peter* got on the line, looking for you."

"He did? Peter did?" He put his glass on the counter. "Shit."

"He said he's coming over here to pick you up." She paused. "I don't know if you remember how much I liked her, Martin, but I liked her a whole lot. She was a sweetheart, and she did you a world of good. You were a wonderful person when you were with her. You were a genuinely good guy. You remember that?" She looked up from the floor, tossing her hair back over her shoulders. "And now you don't even talk to people."

"No," he said. "I'm getting over it, though."

"You like making other people do the work, I think." She cocked her head. "Which is all right, maybe, for now. But I wouldn't make it a habit."

"Yeah."

She wiped some more, then said, "I just came over to make sure you weren't doing anything rash."

"No," he said.

"We don't know what to make of you, Martin."

"You know, I used to talk women into bed," he said, realizing it. "Maybe that's what it is."

She scowled. "Don't try it on me," and continued cleaning. Martin went to the balcony to watch for Peter. He was afraid — who wouldn't be? — but the sound of Maria banging around in the kitchen was a comfort. Probably, he thought, no one would kill him.

Peter drove stiffly, his arms out like poles, his head back against the headrest. His jaw was set; he hadn't shaved, and a fine stubble sanded his cheek. He and Martin rode over the Ballard Bridge, the metal seams banging *ta-ta-ta-ta* against the wheels. "Gotta love this city," Peter said.

"I can't stay out for long," Martin said.

"Yes, you can."

"I've got my freezer defrosting."

"It'll keep."

"I don't want to stain the floor."

Peter changed lanes suddenly, whipping Martin against the door. "You know, I'm cold," Peter said, holding out his hand. "Feel this."

Martin felt it. Cold and stiff.

"I'm a statue," Peter said, gravely. "My circulation is shit. My blood pressure's *dropped* thirty points in six months."

"That's something."

"This is hell," Peter said. "This is it, right here." He gestured at the traffic with his white, bloodless hand and steered onto a side street. "This fucking day-to-day bullshit-nothing life we live. Hell on earth."

"No shit."

"You know, I believe in purposes," Peter said. "I think there are purposes to things. Nothing makes sense otherwise. I sit down at the docks all day and people go in, come out, and I think, Why the fuck am I painting the bottoms of boats that nobody's ever going to see? What the *fuck* am I doing here? But now I know the reason why I'm there."

"What's the reason."

"Because I deserve it. We deserve what we get. I was a fuck-up in school, that's what I get. Jesus, you know what I used to do? I used to play *pool* all day when I should have been in class. I played for money when I was fourteen. Jesus." He shook his head. "Wish I had those days back. I'd go to school like I was supposed to."

"You still could."

"No, it's too late," Peter said, affably. "Too late for me. But it's the old complaint. Never mind." Peter signaled and turned into another side street, this one darker, littered with trash. "Purposes, though. Things happen for reasons. *Most* things, anyway; I don't mean like Evelyn. That's different."

They drove in silence. They passed a boarded-up Ernst, then a warehouse. It started raining.

Peter took in several breaths as if to speak, letting each one out slowly. His fists tightened around the steering wheel.

Martin said, "You're thinking this thing with Josephine."

"Yeah, well, coming into my goddamn *house*, you know? It's on my mind, let me say that."

"Yeah."

"Jesus Christ," Peter said. He rubbed his face. "I mean, *what*. We were both drunk. That's the only reason she told me. She doesn't know half the things she's doing anymore. Hell, I don't. We walk around the house all day drunk and naked. All the shades down. Drunk and naked. I'm drunk now, in fact. I've got to be. Mexico was just — drunk for months."

Martin nodded.

"You don't believe me."

"Sure I do."

"You like thinking about us walking around like that? Naked? I bet you do." He pulled up at the curb and undid his seatbelt. "All right, so you approached her."

"She approached me," Martin said.

"The hell she did," Peter said.

"No, it's true. She put the shirt against me. I mean, we both did it. We were both responsible."

"I want you to understand something," Peter said, calmly. "Okay? You know nothing. You know nothing about me or Josie or anybody. You're a selfish little shit and you always were, okay, and the more I see you, the more pissed off I am that my daughter ever met such a monumental piece of horseshit as you."

"You're not so great yourself." Martin's hands were shaking.

"*Exactly* what I thought you'd say," Peter said, still calm. He tipped his orange cap back. "Just a little horseshit answer from a little horseshit guy. She was my *world*. *Every*thing. The rest of this is *nothing*." He gestured out the windshield. "Shitty job, shitty weather, shitty car. Shitty house. And the rest of my life I'll be thinking about how she spent those years with *you*" — he began crying, his lips mashed out of shape — "and not *us,* where we would have taken care of her and given her what she deserved."

He punched Martin halfheartedly on the chin; it was without force and didn't hurt. "The rest of my life," Peter said, still crying. "I'm going to be in this city for the rest of my life until I die, and I don't ever want to see you again, not ever, not even by accident or anything."

Martin got out of the truck. He was not sure where he was, but he started walking. He could walk home. He could buy new food.

"Stop," Peter said, climbing out of the truck. "I can't chase after you. My goddamn knees."

Martin stopped and turned toward him.

"I want you to apologize," Peter called across the street.

"For what?"

"For what you did to my wife."

"I'm telling you," Martin called, "it's not what you think."

"Jesus Christ," Peter said, "just apologize. Do me the courtesy."

"I can't apologize for nothing. I didn't do anything."

"You did," he said. "You fucking made a pass at my wife, goddamn you."

"I did not."

"Yes, you *did,* goddammit. You fucking *humped* her, like you humped all those other goddamn women. Apologize. Please. It'll make me feel better."

"All right," Martin said. "I'm sorry. I'm sorry for what I did to your wife." And to his surprise, relief flooded him. He *was* sorry, sorry for Josephine, for all the women, everything. Of course he was. But he was surprised at how good it felt to say so out loud: he could feel his lust abating, a feeling like a wave receding, washing away from him. Happily, he said, "I'm very, very, very sorry. Very, very, very sorry."

"Oh, Jesus Christ." Peter waved his orange cap at him and hobbled back to the truck. "Goddamn you to hell."

"Okay," Martin said, mildly. That was all right too. Full of calm, he stood in the middle of the street. Traffic whished in the distance. Trees stood out against billboards. Paper cups rolled in the gutters.

Peter started the truck.

Martin saw all this, but at the same time he was also seeing, vividly, their house, hanging in the air above the street. It was the real thing —

he knew this as one would know the truth in a dream. Peter revved the engine, his arm hanging out the window, but the house remained, more solid than it had ever been. Curious, Martin examined it: a little blue house with a patchy lawn, in a neighborhood he didn't recognize, a concrete front walk, the front stairs wooden and slanted a little. He knew what was inside: the front hall had two cane baskets, one for his mail, one for hers. He went from room to room, picking things up, setting them down. He stood in the street — Peter drove toward him, and Martin wondered, idly, whether Peter intended to run him down, but he didn't want to move: he was afraid the vision would vanish. Peter drove past, slowly, saying nothing. The house was not like the house he had always imagined: it was smaller, older, shabby; but the carpets in the living room were red and opulent, and her spindly music stand grew in a corner, holding creamy pages of music. And Evelyn was there, too, always in the next room, just around the corner, down the hall. The rooms were full of her. Her presence hung thick in the air, like a sound that had barely faded away, and he went sailing through the rooms, looking for her, though he could never quite catch up to her, and it was frustrating, chasing after her like this. But if this was his hell, to live always in rooms she'd just left — well, he would take it.

It was a moment he would remember for a long time. The house stayed with him for months afterward, just as vivid as it had been there in the street, and at work, answering phones for Halloran, he could walk through it at will — the attic, the basement — an inexplicable gift from the unrealized future. And when it did begin to fade, many months later, he felt Evelyn fading, too. He forgot an upstairs bathroom; he could not imagine the kitchen cupboards; the front hall grew shorter and became shapeless; and this went on until the whole house was nothing more than a vague shape, maybe on a hill. And by then Evelyn was almost gone — and how it saddened him! — until at last she was just an unexpected space in his arms, a place where, when he turned at night in his big square bed, he expected to find her, and found only the empty air.

# A Fair Trade

ANDIE could find no seats in the observation car, so she stood, in the unexpected dome of daylight, grasping a warm pole and watching, through the eastern windows, what everyone else was watching — Fort Ord, announced over the loudspeakers ten minutes ago. It was a disappointment: mile after mile of brown gullies and solitary stones. The train was full of soldiers, but here, upstairs, the seats were taken by old women, young women with babies, a quartet of old men in green suits, all of them gazing at the landscape without comment, the women turning the babies around on their laps to see. They passed a herd of antelope, or what Andie thought were antelope, and a murmur went from one end of the car to the other. The animals, startled by the train, poured single file over a fence and ran uphill, and soon they were gone from sight. "My word," said an old man behind her, "the things you see." Andie, uncharmed, went back downstairs.

But that night she couldn't sleep, and during the slow ride over the Siskiyous she felt, pleasantly, that she was being towed uphill in a long sledge, feet first. Well past midnight the rocking of the train grew severe, and Andie opened her eyes. They were in the middle of a long trestle, suspended over a dark river, and the moon was out above a hill. Black mysterious water poured like oil beneath them. It was all beautiful, and she wanted to climb over the dark folds of the hill and keep walking, but the train swept her slowly away. She was not one to be affected by beauty, or so she thought, but the sight seemed to open a warm hole beneath her breastbone, and she watched for hours until clouds obscured the moon. Over rough track the train's metal doors rattled open and shut, as though people were coming and going, ghostly arrivals and departures among the black hills, and behind her a man was counting, counting, in a voice that barely reached her. Near dawn she stood and walked the length of the car toward the bathroom. One soldier, a small man with a long pointed nose, glanced up, looked her over indifferently, and returned his gaze to the window. It was what she had come to expect. She was fourteen years old, nearly flat-chested, and had a face like the back of a spoon, or so she thought; her father was dead, killed in the Pacific, and her mother had sent her to live with an aunt in Seattle. With all this she believed she cut a tragic figure and was proud to have told no one on the train any of her secrets. When she came back to her seat the old woman next to her pulled in her legs and said, "Oh, excuse me," and let out a thin stream of gas, which smelled briefly like a roast before it drifted away.

On the morning of the third day the train slowed and entered the city. Andie, at the window, saw a harbor full of ships. A series of hills ran down to the water. The old woman next to her, Bella, sat up and sighed. "Well, at last," she said, her cheek quivering under a coat of powder. "The fright of it. I know I'll be a dead woman before I do this sort of thing again."

Andie gathered her things, pulled her enormous suitcase upright.

"I wonder if you would help me for a moment," said Bella. "I wonder if you would take my hand and squeeze, rather, like this." She demonstrated. "I have an awful time with that particular hand."

Andie took the old woman's hand, soft and pliant, and flattened it gently between her palms.

"Oh, my. Oh, dear, do," Bella said. "Precisely. Now this one. Oh, yes, exactly. Oh, exactly. Oh." She closed her eyes, put her head back against the seat. "My goodness," she said at last, and reached into her purse. "And here are three dollars for your trouble."

"I don't need any money."

"Of course you do."

Andie took it and stood with her suitcase. "Anything else?"

"No. I have to meet my sister," said Bella, "and I think I'll just sit and put that off for a while."

Andie made her way to the door. The soldier with the long nose noticed her and touched his hat. "Finally here," he said.

"So we are."

"Meeting someone?"

"Yes. My aunt," said Andie. "Thank you very much."

"Relax," said the soldier. "You're too small to keep."

Andie stepped onto the sunny platform. Immediately she saw her aunt Maggie, standing like a ladder under the iron awning. She was taller than Andie remembered, with sharp elbows, and already she was stepping, high and deliberate, like a stork, through the crowd. She wore brown pants and sandals, and her hair was piled on her head and fixed with a tortoiseshell clip. "Well," she said. "You look a little woozy. My God, what a suitcase. You can live in that, I suppose."

"Sorry. It's all we had."

"Sorry? Forget sorry." Grunting, her aunt took the suitcase and led her away, into the depths of the yellow-tiled station and out the other side, back into daylight. The smell of seawater hung in the air, and a tall white building stood shining in the sun. "I haven't got a car, all right," said Maggie, leading her to a taxi, "so we're taking a cab, and I don't want you to think anything of the expense. There are buses, however, and we don't have to worry about being stuck out in the sticks by ourselves. I myself like to come into town and see a movie now and then, and I'm happy to do whatever you'd like to do, Andie, within reason, of course, though I think you'll find everything to your liking. And so," she said, tending to a stray strand of hair, "I think that's that. You're very tall, you know. You're going to be tall like your grandfather — that's where *I* get my height. You don't remember him, I'm sure."

"Not really."

Maggie sighed, opened the taxi door for her. "No, and more's the pity. Everyone else, you excluded, I haven't much use for."

They rode through downtown, up a hill and down the other side, out to the very northern edge of the city, where the houses, less frequent, finally petered out into farmland and forest. The road narrowed, grew sinuous, and at last they left the pavement entirely and rattled a mile along a dirt road to Maggie's house. It was a small white house set down in a meadow, the porch sagging, the chimney pot perched slightly askew, the driveway a rut in the grass; the house was surrounded by the dark green moat of the garden: flowers in front, vegetables behind, rhododendrons clustered on the sides.

The front hall was dim and smelled peculiar, like burned meat, with a flattish damp smell like old newspapers, and Andie felt a clutch of apprehension. But the house grew brighter as they went through it, and in the kitchen, yellow curtains shaded the windows. She followed her aunt onto a sunny back porch and across the porch to a small white door.

"So, dear," her aunt said, showing her in. "This used to be the storeroom, but I've fixed it up for you. Sorry about that smell, by the way. I found a leg of lamb for us to have tonight but it went up in flames, and then I had to clean the oven, which is not something I usually do. This should be all right for you? You don't need much furniture, I hope."

"No, I love it," Andie said, not altogether insincerely. There was a cot and a white wooden desk, a white chest of drawers, and three windows: one over the bed, two over the desk. Beneath her shoes she felt grit on the floor. A nice room, nicer than she'd had in San Diego. "I absolutely love it."

"Well, you don't have to act like that. It's the only thing I have. I guess you'd like a bath."

"I must look terrible."

Her aunt licked her teeth — in the top row they overlapped one another, left to right — and regarded Andie. "No, you don't. I thought you would, but you don't. You're a little pale, I guess. But, no, you look presentable."

"I would like a bath."

"Well, then, darling, I'll get you some towels," said Maggie, and went off into the hallway.

Andie opened her suitcase on the floor. Inside were her ratty underwear, her hairbrushes and combs, her piles of sweaters — all of them smelling of cooking grease — and her shoes. Like a bird, she lifted one arm, then the other, sniffing her armpits. Through the windows she could see the garden: tomatoes and beans on their poles. The walls of her room were white, and so was the ceiling; only the doorknob, solid black enamel, stood out in the whiteness, like a single period on a page without text.

Later, in the back yard, her aunt knelt on a towel, weeding the flower-beds, her hair in a bandanna. "So, I was thinking, Andie," she said, "I might warn you of a few things around here."

"Shoot." Birds dashed above her, singing.

"Well, first, I work a good deal, and I don't know how *you* are with people, but I, Andie, am *not* very sociable, unlike, say, your mother, so you shouldn't expect to see anyone out at the house. I don't know very many people, and all our relatives keep to themselves, which is fine by me. Oh, look at this. This is botrytis," she said, holding out a leaf. "Mold." It was soft and wet, like bad soap.

"For example," she said, wiping it off, "take the MacEwins across the road, to whom I've spoken exactly three times in the seven years of my life here. You'll want to leave them alone, I think. They're old and sick, and by now they must depend on their man to do just about everything. And there's a nephew out here whom we all try to more or less ignore — Dale's his name — and I haven't seen *him* since Christmas, a young man who makes his own *marmalade* in his spare time, if you know what I mean. He wants in the army but they keep refusing him and then he goes home to make his marmalade. Disgusting stuff, and I've got *closets* full of it, hidden away, and I guess I should just throw it all out but I haven't got the heart. That's not a weed."

"Sorry."

"Dale's your *cousin*, now, he's your uncle's son. Your uncle Bernard, who's in the navy. But not like your poor father. Bernard's on a supply ship or something. Out of harm's way." She shook her head, yanking at the ground. "Of course you've never heard of these people."

"No," she said.

"Well, they're hardly worth the bother." Maggie stood and stretched, her knees cracking, reached into her apron, and pulled out a small pair of silver scissors. "These, Andie, are for flowers. Pick what you want, but these and only these are what you use. Otherwise you'll leave a mark."

So it was with a sense of orderly pleasure that Andie went to bed early, with light still showing through the tops of her three windows. She loved her room, she decided, all her own. She tried to sleep, but the rush of wind through the trees kept her softly awake. Her cot, unsettlingly narrow at first, became quickly the perfect slip of bed, floating above the white floor, where, later, moonlight played its watery patterns through the trees. She could smell the sea. Outside, an animal was scratching, occupied with something. Alone, alone, Andie thought, the world opened. Between waking and sleep she remembered the three dollars in her pocket, and she dreamed, briefly, of the long unpopulated passages of the darkened train.

The next evening they rode into town, to the Neptune Theater, near the university. "I was sorry to hear about your father," Maggie said on the bus, "though he didn't treat you in any overly generous way, in my opinion. Certainly he stepped into harm's way."

"Yes," Andie said; "he wanted to." She felt the leather seats, tough and worn, with little horny patches where they'd been repaired.

"I've been wondering, also, about your feelings toward your mother. If you don't mind my asking."

"Not really."

"I guess I just wonder if you're happier now, away from her. I know I would be, if I were you. She's not the ideal guardian, I mean to say."

"I'm not that sorry to be gone."

"Well," Maggie said, considering, and clicking her shoes together in the aisle. "But, also, you should understand what compels her. She is irresponsible, but given her upbringing it's a little hard to hold it against her."

"She made me do everything," Andie said. And this was true: her mother had done essentially nothing for months, lying in bed for weeks on end, long before her father was killed. It had not been a glamorous life, her mother creeping out to the porch by noon, usually venturing no farther, tucking her clothes around her and sitting to watch the traffic, always dangerously prone to self-dramatization, crying against the shelves in the PX. "She hardly went outside except to go to parties."

"Well, she's done that all her life. All her life, I tell you. She was very upset when your father went out to sea and left her alone. My sister has never been any good at being on her own, Andie. Your father in the navy knew that before he went in, but off he went anyway, leaving the two of you to fend for yourselves."

"He volunteered," Andie said.

"Well, yes. Growing up, your mother just couldn't stand to be unaccompanied. She is terribly lonely without you, but I convinced her it's the best thing for her now, as I believe it is. We may," she said, "telephone her sometime, if you want to. Though there is the expense to consider."

Andie clasped her hands in her lap. She felt obscurely obligated to defend her mother and her father, but in fact she was unsure whose side she should be on. Everyone had acted poorly, as she saw it, and she seemed to have no one left. Her father, a small, often timid man, had talked his way from a desk job onto a battleship, an idiotic posturing for which Andie would never forgive him. "At least I didn't lie around in bed for months and months," she said at last. "I didn't have a crackup even before he died."

"Yes. Though as far as that goes," said her aunt, calmly, patting Andie's hand, "it's good training for being a wife, should you ever care to embark on that particular enterprise."

They reached the top of a hill, where the bus paused, taking on passengers. Andie smelled her armpits again, quickly; then, sitting up straight in her seat, looked ahead and behind, at the long bright city avenues stretching away from them in both directions, the streetlights sparkling in the rain. Despite everything, this filled her with a mild delight, a feeling that they might tip either way. And then they were off again, downhill.

The Neptune, green-walled like a grotto, was full and bustling. Student voices echoed off the tiled walls. The dark lobby was wet and speckled with bootprints, and Andie clung to her aunt. They sat between two long rows of college boys in white sweaters, Andie with her elbows in her lap. She had been to the movies only rarely, and she'd found them excessive, all the noise and bluster once the lights went down. The college boys in their boots cheered the newsreels: Germany retreating, tanks disappearing in puffs of dust. The boys punched each other, raised their heavy arms like clubs, and then, somewhat worriedly, watched the pictures from the Pacific. The room shook and exploded. Soldiers marched, dark and gaunt in their net-covered helmets. "After this," said her aunt, patting her hand, "we'll have some real entertainment."

Halfway through the news Andie began to cry, thinking of her father. She missed him, but more than that, she felt sorry for his last, bad minutes, drowned or maybe burned alive; she didn't know. His little blue shirts hung in her closet in San Diego, almost too small for her. The music in the newsreels didn't help: the slow marches, the flags half-masted over the endless graveyards. Little white fountains sprang up where pilots fell into the sea. Her aunt clasped her arm in the dark and whispered, "It's soon over, dear," and Andie averted her eyes. Above an exit door stood a lit-up clock, and she watched the minute hand creep thoughtfully around. During the movie the long slope of people around her munched and stirred, and it was mildly discomforting, as it had been on the train, to be among them. Imprisoned in San Diego she'd been obliged to keep one eye on her mother — she'd shopped and cleaned; she'd cooked and emptied the garbage. It was Andie who had opened the telegram, read its three or four formalisms out loud in their yellow, fly-buzzing kitchen, and helped her mother back to bed. Only a month ago, she realized, with some surprise.

On the long ride home, houses gave way to stretches of weeds and brambles. They were the last to leave the bus, and they walked the open road home. A wind had begun, sliding downhill past them to the lake, bringing with it the smell of summer grass. "Well, I feel bad about what I said earlier, so I should add," said her aunt, "that your father, whatever his faults, had a very nice way about him, I remember, a pleasant smile, and he was always kind to your mother, despite everything. He was a gallant man and a good sport, and had no shortage of friends, because he was a good man, and everyone liked him. You have nothing to be ashamed of concerning your father." They were approaching the house, dark in its green cloak. "Yes, I always did like your father," her aunt said, and opened the gate. "But more's the pity, I guess."

Her aunt, an accountant at the Sand Point Naval Station, walked to work in the mornings, and Andie walked most of the way with her, down the dirt road, past farms and gardens, up a little hill and down the other side. The base, on Lake Washington, was a set of low brown buildings, and from the top of a rise they could see a runway where potbellied airplanes sat awaiting repair. "They don't *do* an awful lot of things at this place," said her aunt, swinging her arms. "We watch expenses, you know — gasoline and coffee and what-not. It's a pretty dull job, I have to admit, though I do like the airplanes."

Andie asked whether she had met any pilots.

"Oh, well, they're a sorry crew, most of them, incapable of writing their own names. Farm boys. My humble and contrary opinion is that if you want a real man, you should look in the civilian population. If I were to look for someone, that's certainly where I'd go. Not that they don't ask me, of course. The pilots. Thank you very much. I am not unbeautiful, I believe."

"You're very pretty," Andie said. It was more true than not. "Men ought to be falling all over you."

"Oh, don't think you have to say that sort of thing, Andie. I'm perfectly capable of judging things myself. My awful teeth, for example. Like a poker hand. But it's very sweet of you to say."

After these walks Andie liked coming back to her aunt's orderly house in the grass; it was still July, and she had little to do. She spent the mornings on a blanket in the sunny garden, with the radio through the kitchen window for company, and when after a few weeks she became bored with the garden — and by then she was as brown as a glove — she began exploring; first, beyond the hedges, where the yard opened into a field; then farther, into a black wall of pine trees, where the air was cool and the earth soft under her shoes. Deep within these trees she found a clearing, and in the middle of the clearing was an old tree on its side, stripped of its branches and bark, now silvering in the open, smooth and good to sit on. Around her the woods receded into their mild dimness, and above her hung a ragged circle of sky. Now and then an airplane crossed over, low, on its landing course toward Sand Point, its propellers feathering the air and its metal seams visible from below. Grasshoppers leaped from the weeds and she let the insects crawl on her arms, spitting their juices and swiveling their pea heads, intricate creatures. It was all marvelous to her, really; this, she thought, was what she had missed: these long days, with nothing to do, and no one around.

So her days were empty by design.

Sometimes she wrote a letter to her mother, though she hadn't much to say. Her white room baked dry in the afternoon sun and smelled lightly of paint. She thought occasionally of the soldier with the long nose and the old gaseous woman, both now perhaps dead, a strange and exciting idea. What she believed for weeks to be a train whistle was, according to her aunt, the horn of a ferry on the lake, the midday run to Juanita. Her aunt's bedroom was uninteresting: familiar photographs, her aunt's underwear in the top drawer, old and fragile but otherwise run-of-the-mill. The closets held the usual things and smelled benignly of cedar, though one closet was filled entirely with hats and hatboxes. On a hot day the dim hallways were cool, and little black flies traced ovals in the air, from the hall window around to the screen door, where they threw themselves with what seemed unusual vigor toward the bright, unreachable yard. A fan in the living room whirred all day, tilting the lampshades. Now and then a car went by on the road, kicking up gravel.

All these things Andie loved.

Then one afternoon at the end of August she crossed the road and walked onto the MacEwins' farm.

The farmhouse stood a good way back from the fence, and she was able to avoid it, sneaking up a rutted side road a hundred yards to a stand of maples, where she was hidden from view. When the road ended, in the middle of a field, she turned and made her way through the grass until she was a safe distance behind the farmhouse, the back of which was shabby and unpainted. She saw an outhouse and pig-pens, and after a moment an old woman in a bright green dress came from the outhouse and walked forcefully across the yard, patting her hair. She turned to say something to the pigs before disappearing inside, and the sharp crack of the screen door reached Andie a second late. Soon a man with a mustache appeared around the corner of the house, dark, foreign-looking, wearing a suit jacket and carrying a shovel. He was a handsome man, well built, his hair longish, nearly to his collar. He too spoke to the pigs, then rested his shovel carefully against the side of the house, sat heavily on the back step, and lit a cigarette.

"Yes, the MacEwins, he and she," said her aunt that night, setting out plates, "are two hundred and three hundred years old, respectively. Irish, I believe, though perhaps Scottish, I'm not certain. They have a man, whom you saw, who is either Armenian or Turkish — at any rate, he hasn't got much English, his name is something like Tvarik, I guess. And the MacEwins have an enormous parcel of land, eight or nine acres or something, absolutely unused, all of it, except for those pigs, and I think they used to run horses but that was years ago, when I first moved here. I would just avoid them, dear. Not that they'd harm you, but seen up close they are not a healthy sight. *Caked* with filth. Children of the earth, shall we say. And that man of theirs. Hardly leaves the place."

But in bed that night Andie imagined kissing him, not by any means the first man she had imagined though the first in a while, the first since she had come north. The first foreigner. How her mother shrieked when she brought him home. My husband, she said, pulling up the shades in her mother's room. Here we are.

Andie started school in September, and it began to rain. She walked a mile to the bus over the muddy road, and she was pleased to see she was the only person at her bus stop. She sat up front, doodling on the fogged window. She was in the ninth grade, and, as the new girl, was cautious.

Most fathers, Andie learned, were not overseas but were stationed in Florida or Georgia, or at work in one city or another, far away but out of danger, and in the halls these fathers' letters were handled conspicuously, like money. Some fathers worked in factories, and a few were sick or old. But only Andie's father had died, and everyone knew it. When she'd stood to introduce herself the first day, patting back her hair compulsively, she'd told her classmates about her father, without meaning to, really — that he had died in the Pacific when his ship was hit by a torpedo — and in the small damp room the class had fallen silent, thinking of sharks and bobbing white hats, the things Andie herself had worn threadbare with imagining. And after her father's death was known, it turned out to be a way of distinguishing herself. As though saddened by the weight of her life, Andie ate her lunch at the far end of the lunchroom and lingered in the library during breaks, sharpening her pencils and watching the librarian out of the corner of her eye. Unfriended, she spoke when spoken to, which was rarely.

With such capital she could probably have insinuated herself into one crowd or another: the smart girls, for whom she would have ironed her hair and adopted a cynical twist of the eyebrows, girls who gathered like crows on the steps of the school, frowning at one another — but they were not popular, not at all. The popular girls rouged their cheeks so their faces were lost in a soft red focus, and Andie could have done that with some practice, but their indifference was inimitable, their false womanly talk:

"Oh, Carol, don't be such an ignoramus."

"You cannot be talking to me, dear."

And Linda Sorelson would say, "Darling. *Too* much."

Andie couldn't do that, not in a thousand years; she'd kill herself first. At lunch the popular girls clogged the white bathrooms and gave off their heavy smells and took pictures of one another with their little brown cameras, and at lunch they sauntered down the hallways with boys draped over their shoulders. Andie envied them, a little; the prospect of a boy around her shoulders thrilled her, and she could imagine the weight of his arm, but the boys in her classes were small and childish and had no touch of sorrow to them. She was acting the part of the romantic — she knew that — so she felt she should want more than just a boy; she would need a soldier to look at her, someone older and wiser — Tvarik, say. And maybe with some effort she could have become one of the bad girls, who smoked, who came to class smelling as if they had been rolling in hay, most of them Swedes, big-hipped and milky, who laughed when they made mistakes, and announced their own grades loudly — *Oh my God a C, oh thank God* — and clutched their papers to their breasts, or cried *An F!* and rocked back in their creaking seats and laughed with their hands to their mouths — *Oh my God, my mom's gonna murder me over this, she said if I flunked I'd get a strap.* Andie couldn't imagine these girls beaten — they were so big and loud — but she supposed their parents were bigger and louder, and not to be trifled with. These girls were the children of waitresses and railroad men and had no stories of glory to protect them, but Andie guessed they too played roles and found them as comforting as she did.

But finally Andie belonged to none of these groups and was recruited by none. People pointed her out to friends. She was the new girl, set apart by her particular history and grief. People were supposed to suffer well, and she made sure she did. She was the bereaved;

even the word had a hearty sound to it, like a young brown horse in a paddock.

Then there was a party, and things began to change.

One of the women at the Sand Point Naval Station was to be married, Alice Hudson, and Andie and Maggie dressed themselves.

"You know, they're all married down there," Maggie said in the front hall, hands on her hat, looking into the mirror. "This Alice Hudson was my last bulwark and now off she goes, no one but a bunch of little babies playing kiss-the-soldier and here I am, out in the country with all my hats and no husband to look after me. Not that I want one. You know what they call me? They call me the Giraffe, thank you very much. With friends like that."

"You don't have a husband to boss you around," said Andie, "and they're jealous of it."

"Well, that's one way of putting it. Cruelty to animals is closer, I think. You're going to be exposed to some foolishness here, and don't blame your aunt if your aunt indulges herself somewhat — God knows there are few enough opportunities. And it's Alice Hudson's booze, and she owes me, especially now."

The naval station was dark, as it always was at night. Each guardhouse, like a little tollbooth, was lit by a single, dim lamp, the upright interior shadowed, the guard nodding them in after examining their purses. Andie saw two airplanes behind guard, on the runway — complicated black shapes — before she and Maggie entered one long brown building and then another, traveling down a hallway toward the sound of music and laughter. "Now," said her aunt, as they rounded a final corner, "if at any time you wish to vanish and so forth, you say the word and we shall absolutely *vanish*. I don't want you feeling you've got to stay for my sake. There are, I must tell you, going to be a certain number of *men* here. Say what you will about that, but you stay clear of them, if you please. You are much too young to do anything beyond having a nice talk, and please don't make your old aunt worry about you. They may try something, who knows, and naturally if *that* happens we will leave immediately. But most of the men here are old enough to be, in a very real sense, your father, which is how you ought to think of them, even if they look at you and see something entirely different and not at all a daughter."

Andie, feeling a little exposed, said, "They're all after you."

"Well, they might be," said her aunt, straightening her hat once more, "and I think at my age and situation that's just fine."

The room, with the desks shoved aside, was bright with noise. Music came from a turntable in the corner. A clutch of women drank beer from brown bottles, and here and there Andie saw men, some in uniform, one of them with a long narrow nose, familiar-looking but not quite the man from the train. In the middle of the room stood a white pillar, and a man and woman danced on either side of it, facing each other. The man, dressed in an ordinary green suit, made feints at the woman, who danced with her eyes closed.

"That would be Alice," said her aunt, "with her friend. Oh, for heaven's sake, look at them. That would be the notorious Richard Enger." She introduced Andie around: women with powder on their collars, hair falling astray, names Andie didn't catch until she came to Greta, blond, at the end of the line, who took her hand and stared at her. "Oh, Andie," said Greta. "You look just like your aunt. Such a grown-up looking girl."

Andie, embarrassed, said, "Thank you."

"Do you dance?"

"No," Andie said, though she had always wanted to. "I never learned how."

"Would you like a beer? Have a sip of mine."

Andie shook her head, though in fact she had been drunk once, alone one day in the house in San Diego, and had hidden the two unmissed bottles deep in the garbage. "No, thank you," she said — childishly, she thought. She glanced around for her aunt.

"You must be awfully sad about everything, Andie. I'm so sorry. Your father. And you so young."

"My aunt has been very nice," she said.

"My brother-in-law died, you know." Greta gripped Andie's arm, her lips coming loose as though she was about to cry. "So awful. All the poor men."

Her aunt was dancing with a small man wearing a yellow tie, his squarish head hard and burled like a hazelnut.

"Oh, now, *that* man, Andie, is your aunt's boyfriend. Harrison Beam."

Andie said, "Her boyfriend?"

"Well, more or less. It depends on her. He'd marry her in a flash. And she's always complaining about how she's such a poor so-and-so and never gets a date. She was so cruel to poor Alice Hudson, who never wanted anything but exactly what she has right now." Greta looked speculatively at Maggie. "Your aunt, you know, has very strict standards."

Her aunt, dancing, had put her white hat on a table, and Harrison Beam, rolling the round nut of his head, was holding both her hands.

"Now," said her aunt afterward, on the dark warm road, "I guess I never told you about him. He is usually a very nice man, but he has this terrible mean streak. He can be cruel if you catch him at it, and has a stable of women, so I'm not the only girl he dances with. I think there's some little thing he's trying to marry somewhere else, or anyway he makes these *comments*, I guess you'd call them, which is why, despite everything — well, despite everything I might like, there is little danger of being swept off my feet, Andie, not that Harry's the sweeping type in the first place." She folded her hat, unfolded it again. "Nor, come to think of it, am I. Still. I do like him an awful lot. You think I'm crazy?"

"He likes you."

"I think he does, a little."

"Greta said he wanted to marry you."

"Oh, well. Greta. I'm afraid Greta is not the most reliable source." Harrison worked as a planner for the school board, said her aunt, and he had his eye on the MacEwins' farm; it would be a good spot for a school, according to him, and he was planning to make them an offer. Maggie had met him one day on the road, he with city papers on the hood of his car, and she walking home. "He was what my mother used to call an Unlikely," Maggie said. "But many nice things are just that."

With this, Andie felt free to think of Tvarik as much as she liked. She lingered on the front porch, hoping to see him when he retrieved the afternoon mail from the box at the road. He was dirty: his blue suit jacket showed sprays of mud, his thin black boots, caked, laced far up his ankles. He had a black bicycle and pedaled clumsily up and down the road, arriving home with the saddlebags full — of what, Andie wondered? She felt — was feeling most acutely — her separation from the adult world, even as she approached it. She could not easily imagine what people did in life, minute to minute. Did Greta drink beer in the morning? Did Dale, the marmalade-making cousin, work? And what could his unmentioned job be? When Tvarik vanished into the house she lost him entirely.

But he was, in her fantasies, much younger than he appeared to be, maybe only twenty-two, and his hair, though tacky and thick in life, felt, to her imagined touch, soft and thin, like a child's. He owned a car, gray and old, which he kept under a cloth in a barn; their drives were long, thoughtful, neither of them saying much. They went out beyond the city limits, where Andie had never been. Where trees overhung the road, he steered the car to the shoulder and drew her to him. Alongside the road she imagined fields, and idly, as though finishing a painting, she placed cows here and there, the farthest only white specks on a green hill. Bathing in a river they saw each other naked, admired each other, but that, for now, was all.

And Maggie seemed happier. She talked to Harrison on the telephone — sometimes he called late, after ten — and from her cot Andie would hear her aunt scramble into the hallway, and her voice, softening, would carry indistinctly through the kitchen and out to Andie in her white room. When he arrived to pick Maggie up he sat out in the car, under the trees, and Andie, lurking on the porch, would wave. Harrison, his green arm propped on the open window, would wave back and flash his even teeth. "Howdy," he might say, and gaze down at his dashboard.

"Now, Andie," said her aunt, stepping out for the night in one of her thousand hats, "don't think there's anything serious between the two of us. This is nothing. He has no designs on me. And truthfully I prefer being alone, I really do. This is just a passing thing." Then back went her head. "My throat is fine?"

"You look pretty," said Andie.

"I think I asked you not to say that, sweetheart," said her aunt, mildly, and walked across the grass.

Things around the house became neglected. The hanging ferns turned brown at the edges and lost their leaves; bills piled up; underwear dried for days on the towel racks. Early one morning Andie woke and saw a bobcat in the dim garden, and she slid her window open slowly, but it scooted away, low and matted, and it seemed to Andie a sign, her aunt's recent distraction sensed not only by her but by the animals and brambles, as if it carried a certain smell. Maggie was out later and later, and Andie would wear her aunt's hats around the dark house, the radio on in the front room while she dusted and scrubbed. It was her house, she decided; she had bought these dishes, arranged this furniture; these magazines were hers, stacked beneath the coffee table; this toilet, with its rust ring, was her own. Then one night in October her aunt did not come home at all, was out all night with Harrison, and Andie walked through the empty rooms, eating from a can of beans and picturing the two of them together: his fingers going down her aunt's dress, burrowing around the edges of her underwear, her aunt's long thin legs opening. In the morning Andie felt the expectant quiet of the house, like a cup held out to be filled.

Her aunt was lying on the sofa when Andie came home from school. "Well," said her aunt, balancing a glass of water on her stomach, "pity poor me, thank you very much. Some aunt I am."

Andie sat down beside her.

"He has those hands." Maggie made a vague shape in the air. "The man hasn't done a hard day's work in his life." She rocked the glass with her fingertips. "Well, not that anything *happened*, not really. Nothing *important*."

"I bet," Andie said.

Her aunt scowled, earnestly. "No, his car overheated, you know, and it turns out he's got a bottle of hooch in the car, so out it comes, and we're waiting for the truck and we just kept *drinking*, which as you know is not really like me, and by the time the truck comes neither of us can stand, hardly. So I spent the night in a motel. Harry and I had separate rooms, thank you very much, so don't think I did anything too untoward. But the clerk, my lord. The maids. I was so mortified this morning I almost didn't come home. I'm sorry I didn't telephone, by the way."

"That's all right. I had some beans."

"Oh, Andie, I'm so sorry. I suppose you're used to this sort of neglect from your mother. You must wonder why you came."

"How's Harrison?"

"Oh, worse. Sick as a dog. So awful. This is why I prefer to make my own entertainments. I never know what not to do." She took a pack of cigarettes from her purse. "And I've begun smoking again, for heaven's sake. I almost wish I'd never met the man. He's encouraged me to do this." She lit a match. "Thinks it's cosmopolitan."

Andie reached for the pack, extracted a cigarette, and put it between her lips. It was lighter than she had anticipated, and tasted like figs. "Mind if I try?"

"It'll make you sick." But Maggie closed her eyes. "Though I don't suppose much else can go wrong."

"I've done it before. Only once," she said. "With some girls. We went out behind the MacEwins' house."

"I'm sure you did."

"We did. They were dancing and drinking hooch."

"Oh, Andie, please don't joke," Maggie said. "There's not a decent brain left between them or they'd have sold that place long ago. I can't mention the amount, but it's outlandish."

"Maybe it's in the will for Tvarik."

"Please," her aunt said, irritated. "Don't start. Harrison would kill them."

"I'll bet it is. They don't have anyone else."

"Well, Andie, I know how handsome that awful Tvarik is to you, and I'm not sure what you have in mind, exactly, but Harrison is determined to get that place, and he's quite amoral. I can attest to that myself. You never know what he's going to do." She pursed her lips and looked down at the length of herself on the couch, adjusting her dress. "So I would reconcile myself to the fact that those people are not long for this world."

Andie removed the cigarette from between her lips, examined its moist end, and put it back into the pack. Her aunt had closed her eyes and thrown an arm over her face, and now she looked much like her sister, haggard and drawn, her cheeks beginning to pouch and the powder showing in creases on her neck. As though Harrison were better looking, Andie thought, angrily. As though her aunt were beautiful.

Thereafter, Harrison came to spend more time around the house, evenings when he sat in the kitchen with the blunt pipes of his legs crossed, his little hands folded over his knee. His small compact head sat handsomely enough on his shoulders, Andie thought, but he smoked a lot and coughed mightily into a gigantic handkerchief, which covered his front entirely, and when he stood, he hitched up his pants. It was a smallness that might have been endearing, a reminder of her father, but, sitting with his jaw tight and his tie knotted, he seemed desperate, like a salesman with a bad territory. His dark eyes were too moist, and from his round nostrils sprouted tufts of wiry hair. He had been wounded, it turned out; he walked with a limp and couldn't raise his right arm over his shoulder. "In a plane crash," he told Andie. "Broke my leg, too."

"In the Pacific," Maggie explained.

"Yes." He shrugged in his slightly overlarge suit. His skin was darkish, nutty. "Caught on fire, the whole thing." Only once did he mention the MacEwins. "Rotting old pigs better off in a home," he said. And always at the end of the evening he would rub his eyes with the four fingers of each hand and then examine his fingers, frowning, saying, "Oh, time, time to go, time to go."

Afterward Maggie cleaned his dishes, stacked them neatly, and said, "I will come to my senses, Andie. I know exactly what you're thinking. But he's really not a terrible man all the way through. And I guess I *do* enjoy his company, a little of it, anyway. You know, before you and he came along all I had was that *Dale*, the marmalade cousin." She wiped the counter and sighed. "He is terrible about those MacEwins. I mean they're real sticks in the mud but he does run them down whenever he gets the chance."

"They don't want to sell," Andie said.

"No, and you can't blame them, can you. But it's only a matter of time before he gets it. His office sends these letters, my goodness, those people probably get more mail now than they ever did." Maggie turned to face her. "So I ought to tell you, Andie, that if and when this does happen, we shall be moving."

"Oh, no," she said. "Moving?"

"Out to Juanita, you know, where that ferry goes. I don't *want* to, exactly, but if there's a school across the street? All those kids? They'll go back in my bushes and start lighting fires and necking and doing who knows what else, the bad ones. Harrison said the school might buy it."

"If they bought it they'd just knock it down."

"Well, I suppose so. You can't get very much for a house like this,

Andie. Nobody wants to live like this anymore. There's a little devel-
opment going up in Juanita. They're not very nice houses, you know,
those flat-roofed jobs, but we could see the lake."

"You'd have neighbors. You'd hate that."

"Well, they wouldn't be right on top of us. And it's a long way from
the city."

"We could stay here," Andie said, though she felt she was begging.
"We could put up a fence."

"Yes, and have them write whatever they'd write on it? No thank
you."

"I like it here," Andie said.

"Don't be ridiculous, dear," said her aunt, turning away. "You can't
possibly."

There were nights they sat around the radio, Andie with her homework, her aunt with her sewing, and Harrison with his magazine,
grunting as he read. He rarely met her glance, and sometimes Andie
stared past him, admiring her reflection in the dark window. Occasionally he would say something out loud. "Fifty thousand tons," he
might say, shaking his head. Or, "Two thousand dead in ten minutes."

Once Andie asked, "How much are they paying for the Mac-
Ewins'?"

Without looking up, he said, "I can't tell you that."

"Why not?"

"Just the rules," he said.

"Can't they put a school someplace else?"

"Andie," said her aunt.

"What exactly is it you *do?*" she asked.

"For heaven's sake, Andie."

"You're not a lawyer."

"No," he said. "You don't have to be a lawyer to do what I do."

"I guess you don't have to be much of anything."

"Andie!" Her aunt scowled. "Apologize."

"Sorry," she said, and got up and went into the kitchen.

Her aunt called after her, "You might do some dishes for a change."

And a minute later in he came, to the sink, where he rested his cup
and saucer delicately on the drainboard, his suit jacket rustling. Then
he moved past her to the refrigerator, where he retrieved two beers,

carrying them both in his left hand, wedged, clinking, in his fingers. On his way out his right hand rested for a moment on her rear, a strong hand for its size; she could feel it curve to match her curve. He seemed to feel for heft, and squeezed, and Andie, standing still, wondered for a second exactly what he was doing. "You're getting fat" was all he said before going back to the living room.

It was not the first time such a thing had happened to her — a man on a bus in San Diego had brushed her little breasts with the back of his hand — so she was not surprised, exactly, to have it happen again. Certainly she had seen it everywhere around her, on buses and trains, in the rearmost aisles of stores, an awkward business to watch, awful in its slow approaches and retreats. The women never looked up, just drifted away, as though distracted by the thought of something they'd forgotten to do, and the men, off they went, briskly, not glancing around. The man who had brushed her breasts, a young man, balding, his ears oily and small, got off calmly at the next stop, bought a newspaper, and lit a cigarette, and when the bus rolled on again he began his brisk walk alongside it, keeping pace for a moment, and Andie watched him slide by as though he were a character in a movie, feeling she was supposed to hate him, that he had been chosen for his loathsome role because of his dirty ears. And Harrison — she should have seen it coming, she thought; that head of his.

She turned off the water and walked outside, into the nighttime back yard, and around the dark side of the house to the road in front, which was empty. She crossed it, passed the MacEwins' mailbox, and walked up their drive.

It was a cool night, overcast, and the dark house hung before her. Tvarik's black bicycle sat by the stairs. She felt its worn leather seat, ran her fingers over its ridges and humps, the long suggestive point in front, the wiry underside. Clutching her hair to one side, she leaned to sniff at it, and smelled only leather.

There was light coming from the back of the house, and she walked toward it.

As she moved around the side of the house her feet began to sink in muck, and she heard the pigs sighing disappointedly in their pens. Behind her she heard the wind rushing downhill to the lake, as it always did, shushing through the trees. Then through a window she saw them all, the three of them, as if on stage: Mr. MacEwin, ancient,

mouth agape, head back, asleep as if dead in a chair; Tvarik, himself
stooped and undeniably old, his face creased and leathery, standing,
combing a curly brown wig on his fist, turning it this way and that.
Watching him from a chair was Mrs. MacEwin, bald as a baby, eyeing
the wig as if it were a child. Tvarik spoke, and Mrs. MacEwin smiled
bashfully, looked at the floor. He was a small man, too, Andie saw, but
nothing like she'd imagined. Leaner, happier. She could take a bus, she
thought, and be on the train in the morning, be in San Diego in two
days. Instead, she walked along the dark road until her feet began to
hurt, out to the darkened base and back, and by the time she got
home, Harrison had left and her aunt had gone to bed.

After this, she was not sure what to do. Harrison acted as though
nothing had happened, still sat grunting at his magazines. She wasn't
sure her aunt would believe her, so she said nothing.

But at school that week she stole Linda Sorelson's camera. It was
easy, and she did it almost accidentally: took it from beneath Linda's
desk at lunch, hid it under rags in a janitor's closet, picked it up after
school, and covered it with her coat on the bus home. Linda didn't
miss it for two days, and by then it was sitting on Andie's desk at
home, where it unnerved her, this brown box, though to her surprise
she felt no remorse. Linda Sorelsen was one of the popular girls and
accepted the theft with gallant school-yard dignity and a little sneer;
there would be better things for her later on, she seemed to say.

Andie brought Linda's roll of film to a drugstore downtown, and,
using the three dollars hidden in the satiny pouch of her suitcase, had
it developed: Linda's friends standing at their lockers; the interior of a
white bedroom; a yard, sunny, with flowers. This last was particularly
appealing: it looked like a place where quiet, reasonable things happened, where drinks, as they did in movies, appeared on trays. Or the
people not shown in the picture were out to lunch, driving their own
cars. When they returned, they would give one another smart nods,
say, Yes, how true, a good point.

But she never took pictures of her own and soon she hid the
camera under her cot and tried to forget it. She could believe, most of
the time, that it had nothing to do with her. When she remembered it,
she had a sense of things slipping beyond her control. Maybe this was
how her aunt felt these days, too: that if she could start over here, or

here, her life would become again what it had been, righteous and un-complicated.

Then it was November, and raining constantly. Water ran down the insides of Andie's walls and seeped through the plaster. The rich smell of the yard — moss and earth — met her in the short afternoons after school, in her damp room, where she kept the window open to the chill. These cold hours became Andie's own time, and she felt, faintly, the same languor she had felt during the summer, with the cool house empty around her, the wet fields unpopulated on all sides, though now her white room ticked with rain and the air was filled with the smoke of wood fires, and the rhododendron leaves tipped downward in the cold. They were happy hours, when she experienced a sort of nostalgia for her first true self, those summer days alone, with the flies in the house. But when her aunt came in, jabbering, peeling the scarf from her hair, this sensation vanished, and Andie hated her freely and wanted her gone.

This was a reckless feeling, and a hopeless one, and even as she knew it was childish she flounced around the house and spoke desul-torily and washed only her own dishes, and she lied. She skipped school and spent time downtown, roaming the waterfront to see the trains disgorge their khaki soldiers. Many of them spoke to her, bob-bling around her three at a time, and she ducked away, frightened but smiling and unable to help herself. Most of all she loved walk-ing from block to block, hearing the bustle of things but herself aloof, one of the wounded, making her way. When she came home from such a day, she was calm, vigorous, and her loathing of Harrison was stronger.

One night, with the three of them around the radio, Andie said, "I was over talking to Tvarik this afternoon."

"In the rain, Andie," said her aunt.

"I was walking home and he came up to me," Andie said. And why not? He could have, and he may have wanted to, her blue dress, her black hair neat enough in its band. "He was this close."

They waited.

"What did he do?" Harrison asked.

"We had a nice conversation," she said. "I think he's very hand-some."

"He didn't do anything?"

"No."

"He didn't make advances toward you in any way?"

"Well," she said, with plummeting despair, "he said I was pretty, and that he wanted to see more of me, and that I should wear more makeup, and that he thought I'd be a good dancer. He'd seen people like me before and they always turned out to be good dancers."

"Fat chance," said Harrison.

"Now," said Maggie.

"You shouldn't be talking to strange men like that," Harrison said.

Andie smirked and stared at him until he looked back at his magazine. "Shouldn't I?" she said, and got up and left. Behind her she could hear them talking in low speculative voices, the way teachers talked to one another before calling someone's name, or taking someone out for punishment.

That night at her painted desk she wrote to her mother, the first time in weeks. *Dear Mother,* she began. *There is much to tell.* She had a boyfriend, she said, named Marek, a new boy, a refugee, black-haired and quiet, whose voice was so soft the teacher couldn't hear him; Andie had to repeat the things he said. She'd got an A in science, true; she'd been voted secretary of the class, not true. It was late, and her letter grew longer and more elaborate: the voting had been close, and the runner-up was her best friend; her aunt had begun knitting and was trading socks for sugar; she had gone downtown and bought a book of poems, in a green cover, called — and she thought a long while before deciding — *The First Flower.* The garden grew darker, and the moon came out, lighting the muddy paths among the cabbages.

Then, through the kitchen and the back porch, came her aunt's voice, angry: "Well, good for you, Harry. That's very good. Very professional of you."

"He might have done it," said Harrison. "She was over there, right? You should've seen his face. You could see he wanted to."

"You tiny little stupid son of a bitch," said her aunt. "You stupid little man."

After a moment, Harrison replied, with great satisfaction, "You cunt. You cunt, you cunt, you cunt."

There came a long silence; then Andie heard Harrison's car start and drive off.

A minute later her aunt appeared in the back yard. She began weeding the damp winter garden, crouching on the grass. She looked unwieldy, somehow, her hips too wide, her hair undone, in the darkness a furious figure, tearing at the earth with both hands. Her back, illuminated, rolled and pitched beneath her dress. *Your sister is in the garden,* Andie wrote. *She is as pretty as you but in a different way. I believe your sister is sweet on a certain man, but I shouldn't mention it. She wouldn't appreciate my prying eyes. He is a nice man with a car, but at the moment you could say things are a little stormy.*

Her aunt now sat down in the mud, lay back, and looked at the dark sky. Her dress lifted to her knees, white and waxen. She began to cry. Andie dug into her drawer and found a picture of Linda's friends and an envelope, and sealed the picture with the letter. *Meet my friends!* she wrote on the flap. *They're not as bad as they look.*

The next morning her aunt walked to work as though nothing had happened; Harrison never returned. Maggie, in fact, never spoke of him. It was as if he had never been. Then Tvarik disappeared — at any rate, Andie stopped seeing him — and in February the MacEwins were driven away in a white car, and a crew of surveyors arrived; other men — older men, Andie saw, from the porch — tore down the MacEwins' house, threw the boards into the back of a truck, and, wearing leather chaps, cut down tree after tree.

Something had happened, but her aunt, cool and distant, would say nothing — "I don't want to talk about that" — and after a while Andie stopped asking. Her aunt was quieter, and Andie missed her strange talkativeness; but when spring came, and the warm fields opened again on all sides of the house, Andie felt the familiar languor, and it made her feel at home, if nothing else did, as the men across the road dug and poured concrete and backed their trucks over the grass.

Their new house in Juanita was clean and dustless, with avocado draperies, a stone floor in the hallway, and no walls, just partitions here and there. It was an airy place — they moved in July — and Andie, feeling as if she were a visitor, missed her white room. She wondered whether she had stayed too long. But her aunt was happier, and the lake below the windows, a gray plate, was surrounded by trees.

Then, in August, Andie, wandering downtown, saw Tvarik. He was working at a fish market, wearing a rubber apron and a flat blue cap, pushing ice with a broom. He didn't see her, and she turned quickly and walked on. She thought of his bicycle, his sinewy hands. Was he happier here, tossing fish like logs across the counter, his hands red from the ice? And how had he ended up here?

When her aunt came home from work, Andie said she'd seen him.

"Well," her aunt said.

"He looked good."

"Good."

"I didn't talk to him," Andie said. "I don't think he saw me at all."

"But he looked all right?"

"He looked happy," Andie said.

Her aunt hung her hat in the hall closet. "Well," she said, "I suppose you must be wondering."

"Yes," Andie said.

"You can't tell your mother any of this, all right? Please. She'll start to worry about me."

"I won't."

"You promise?"

"Yes."

"All right. Harrison told that man to stay away from you."

"Told Tvarik?"

"Yes. That's what he did. He threatened to go to the police and say that man had attacked you." She lit a cigarette. "So."

"He said that?"

"He did. He'd have done it, too. He knows people. He'd have had that man arrested."

"In order to get him to move?"

"I didn't want to tell you, Andie, it was too horrible."

"He did that?" She thought of his hand on her rear. "What a creep."

"I told you he had a cruel streak." Her aunt shrugged. This was how things worked; people behaved like this; there was fear and cunning. "Yes, he was going to do just that, get that poor man sent to prison, and I have no doubt he could have done it with very little trouble. So of course the man *left* — who wouldn't, for heaven's sake? And once he was gone, the MacEwins were easy pickings. So now you know why I couldn't see Harrison anymore."

"Thank God."

"Oh, I guess so." Standing in her purple dress in the middle of the stone floor, smoking, her aunt seemed altogether alone. "But it goes to show. Dealing with strangers." And the warm spot, surprising her, opened again under Andie's breastbone, and filled with gratitude. They were both happier alone, Andie thought: they were that kind of people.

Andie went back to her mother at Christmas, boarding the same train that had brought her north, and traveling, in the snow and cold this time, over the Siskiyous and down the long green interior of California. The windows of the train fogged, and when it was dark, at five in the afternoon, she slept in her seat, waking at midnight to find the windows clear and the sky full of stars. The observation car was empty of all but a single soldier, who sat at the far end, smoking. Andie sat beside him, and when he offered a cigarette she took it and sucked at it delicately, smoking it to the end. A blue cloud collected beneath the glass dome. The dark winter landscape rolled by outside, and Andie, heady, felt it as the slow turning of the earth itself, as though the banging and shaking of the train were the vast iron machinery of the world. She would always find beauty in the things she saw alone, she knew, and when a year later her mother moved them north, to Portland, she found she liked the rain and the domestic smell of the fertilized garden in the damp mornings; her little bedroom beneath the roof caught the tapping rain, and as Andie grew older, this sound accompanied her studies, and the mumblings of the illicit boys she brought home once in a great while.

Andie found she missed her aunt, her solitary vigor; her mother came home from work dragging her purse on the wet sidewalk. Andie thought often of Maggie and wrote, imagining her, fondly, alone with her hats and new draperies, riding the bus to the movies with her feet in the aisle. Her aunt's letters back were sometimes only a sentence or two: *Two new trees today, out on my knees until dinner.* Or, *Man came to the door selling rope. I don't need rope, I said. You never know, he said. You expect me to hang myself out here, I said. Scared him off.* Over the

years Andie became bolder and more extravagant in her letters, so
when she lost her virginity in college, she was up early the next morning at her desk, to the boy's puzzlement, seated in the vinyl-covered
desk chair, writing and wearing only her underwear. Her aunt wrote
back infrequently after this, and Andie was sure she had crossed a line,
though she hadn't meant to. Two years later she found herself hesitant
to mention her marriage, so she played it down, said it made no
difference; she and Ben could go on forever without marriage, but
there were the presents to think of, and they could use some new
dishes. It was intended as a joke, but she and Ben were divorced soon
enough, leaving Andie with a child, a girl, with whom she moved east,
to Boston. Believing she had not been cut out for marriage, Andie
started over, in a new city, with her daughter. Almost without meaning to she stopped writing to her aunt, even while Maggie lived in a
corner of her mind, wearing those soft hats now long out of style,
a silly figure but one Andie thought of with love, someone who had
tried to make her way by herself before it was really possible to do so.

But Andie could do it. When her daughter left for college, Andie
began to walk long distances around the city, alone, back and forth
across the Charles; the few friends she had outside work she allowed
to fade and finally vanish from her life. She spent evenings in her
apartment and learned to cook well, and taught herself what a good
wine was like, once in a great while spending the night with a man.
It turned out to be a life she loved. She became, and she knew it,
self-regarding. She would rather imagine people than be with them,
but she was fairly sure this had always been true; certainly Ben had
been better in the abstract than in the flesh. But it was difficult to
remember what her life had been like before Boston; it seemed to her
she had always been a solitary girl. During the months with her aunt,
she thought, she had perhaps become that person for good — the
house and fields had worked their alchemy on her — but in the reg-
ular and mostly satisfying whirl of her solitary days, Andie had forgotten, as most people do, much about her childhood, though certainly not by design.

When Andie was fifty-five she moved back to Seattle, as many others
were doing. Her aunt, she learned, was still alive, now seventy-eight.

The city had changed entirely. Even from the air — perhaps especially — the changes were obvious: the new denser sprawl of things, many of the old empty places filled in. Downtown, once squat and marine, was now as glassy and enterprising as Houston or Charlotte, and it saddened her to see that so much of what she had known was gone for good. Her work — after her divorce, she had worked in computers — was bringing her here, and soon she bought a house, revived what had been an elaborate garden in the fenced back yard, and settled down to what she expected would be the last, longest chapter of her life. She did not call Maggie, though she meant to; she lived much as her aunt had lived, and there were days when she would look at the telephone guiltily and chide herself for not calling. But eventually this passed and she could gaze out at her yard or through her wooded window at work and feel she had taken care of everything. Now that she had money, she found it a pleasure to eat well and some nights to drink too much and sit in her bathtub among the green tiles and listen to the radio. Her daughter, in Dallas, was married and rarely visited, and Andie was by far the oldest woman at work in a business populated by men not yet thirty. Her husband, she thought with some satisfaction, would be useless here. Goaded by the youth around her, she ran regularly around Greenlake and bought a fancy bicycle, and she whirred happily through the streets, though her knees hurt and the seat was hard and too narrow.

Then one night, watching television with the lights out, she saw Harrison Beam, an old man, interviewed from his wheelchair. The round nut of his head was pale, he had lost his hair, and his smooth voice was broken and uncertain. He had gone on, she learned, to design parks in the city, parks that were now in danger of being built up. It was a terrible thing, he said, and Andie, curled comfortably under a blanket, agreed with him. He was sweet, harmless. He put her in mind of her aunt, whom she called the next morning, a Saturday. When she offered to take her aunt to lunch, Maggie, speechless for a moment, said, "Oh, it's *Andie*. Well, I wondered when you'd be back."

When the doorbell rings Andie is surprised to find not only Maggie but a man, introduced as Dale, in a blue suit and a yellow tie, a big white block of head. "*You* remember," says Maggie, who is bent and old, wearing a raincoat over her shoulders like a shawl. "*Dale*. The marmalade boy."

"We've never met," says Dale. Dale, maybe sixty-five, blue-eyed, is obviously a gay man. "You were around, but I never met you."

"No," says Andie. "How do you do?"

"I'm fine, thank you."

"Well," says Maggie, gazing balefully at her rubber boots, "I have not in fact become a milk farmer, though I appear to be one. You can afford this house?" She stands in the front room, surprised. "You must be rolling in it."

"I'm doing well."

"Computers," says Dale.

"Yes."

"Good for you," he says. "I'm frightened of the things. I'm afraid I'll press a key and it'll just all blow up, kablooie. I should get over it, I know."

Andie has no patience for such fear, finds it, strangely, womanish. "I can give you a tour if you'd like," she says.

Maggie says, "Well, yes. You ought at least to show me around. You know, my place is just the same. I've been there since you left and you wouldn't believe the malls and what-not they've thrown up around me, it's just awful." They mount the stairs, Andie holding her aunt's arm, Dale following. Her aunt's boots squeak on the floors. They examine the bedrooms, the bright bathroom; Maggie uses the remote on the stereo, disbelieving. "Oh, for heaven's sake. *This* would save a lot of trouble, wouldn't it? You're the only one here, I see."

"Yes, I am. We divorced a long time ago, you may remember."

On the way downstairs, her aunt sits on a chair on the landing. "I," she says, "am going to take a little spell here."

Andie is taken with a sudden fear that her aunt will die there; she is so frail and small, lost in her sweatshirt. Dale says, "Margaret, see what happens when you don't sleep enough?"

"And I've told you, Dale, that I *can't* sleep." She lifts her boots to look down at the carpet. "This thing must have cost a bucketful."

But in the car she does fall asleep, her face in the sun. Andie glances over to be sure she's breathing, and she is. Dale, from the back seat, says, "She was very excited to hear from you, Andie. She couldn't sleep at all last night. I was up at six and she was sitting doing her crossword and *smoking*. I said, Maggie, you can't smoke, and she said, Dale, I'm an old woman, I can do what I want now."

"You live with each other?"

"Oh, yes," says Dale, plumply. "She adopted me some years ago."

"Adopted you?"

"Yes," he says. "Twenty years ago. I am her son."

"Oh," says Andie. "And what do you do, Dale?"

"I am retired from the baking business. I was a baker."

"Oh," she says again. She can think of nothing more to say. It strikes her that her aunt, after all, may be gay. She asks Dale.

"Maggie? No, no," he says, shrugging in his seatbelt. "Unlike yours truly. In case you haven't noticed."

Chinook's, the restaurant, is wide and airy. Silver ventilation pipes run along the high ceiling. The big windows look out on the marina, where blue-painted trawlers and seiners are docked, bobbing up and down.

After a minute of silence Dale says, "Well, Maggie is very excited to see you again, Andie."

Andie smiles. "So am I."

"It was nice of you to call," says her aunt, "after so long."

"I've thought of you often. I'm sorry I stopped writing."

"Oh, well. I had Dale."

"Good," Andie says, but her aunt is up and heading for the bathroom.

"Just a minute," she says, and hobbles off, briskly.

"She has a bladder thing," says Dale when she's gone. "Just a little one."

"I see," Andie says, and Dale keeps talking. His old bakery now a dry cleaner's; the traffic and the freeways; the cost of houses. But Andie doesn't listen. Things, she feels, are a little bit off. Over the years she's imagined what her aunt's life might have been had she married Harrison, bought his whiskey, built his deck. Or if, instead, she'd somehow married Tvarik. Andie's had these fantasies about her aunt — or *for* her aunt, it must be. Maggie goes to Europe in her dotage, visits Armenia — after she is widowed, say — and climbs the brick hill cities, sees the white plazas, the glowing sea; she visits his village, drinks wine in the cafés in the afternoon, eats sesame bread, watches the women shopping — or whatever it is they do there — in the square. And does Tvarik's family appear around her, cousins long forgotten, enemies curious to learn his final, perhaps glorious, certainly American fate? Andie could think these things, could have such hopes for her aunt, knowing that Maggie was in fact at home, by herself, growing older and collecting newspapers, having little accidental fires on the stove. But Dale. She never imagined Dale.

"I saw," Andie says when her aunt returns, "someone on television the other day. It was Harrison Beam, you remember him?"

"Oh, yes," says her aunt, picking at her food.

"You do, don't you? He looked all right, considering."

"That guy must be over eighty by now."

"I think they said he was eighty-two."

Maggie takes a breath. "Should be *dead* by now, the way he lived."

Andie says, "He was pretty handsome."

"Oh, he was not. He was weasely."

Andie, gallantly, says, "He was handsome, and so was that Armenian man, you remember?"

"Oh, for heaven's sake, I'd completely forgotten about him. Across the road. That dirty man you loved so much."

"You didn't forget about him. My first love."

Dale, addressing his water glass, says, "Amen to that."

"Until now I forgot completely," says her aunt. "It's so long ago, Andie. For heaven's sake."

"It doesn't seem long ago."

"Well, it is."

"I thought you wanted to marry Harrison."

"No. Never."

"Never?"

"No," says Maggie. "I said as much at the time, I'm sure."

"I think I didn't believe you."

"Well. Dale believes me."

"Of course I do," says Dale.

Maggie says, "Boyfriends, yes. Marriage, no. No strings."

"She has a boyfriend now," Dale says.

"Oh?"

"Yes, he's seventy-two, very old for a boy. He's a doctor," Maggie says, "and he still practices."

"Handsome, too," Dale says. "For such an old dude."

Andie finds herself laughing. "Good!"

Maggie says, "I don't suppose you have one."

"No. Once in a while, you know. But nothing serious. Not for years."

"Oh, Andie. You ought to. Stirs the blood." She lifts her face to show her cheeks. "Note the complexion."

It is a long lunch, and Dale talks a good deal. Her aunt, after a while, subsides, and sits docilely behind her lunch, clicking and sighing, like a clock tower whose bells have been taken down. Her teeth, Andie sees, are false, and no longer overlap.

And Andie finds she has little to say. What can be said, after so many years? She had, she sees, misjudged her aunt. Andie has given up certain things in life, and it saddens her, a little. She has faint hope of marrying again; she looks forward only to twenty years of her bathtub, her house, the figuring and refiguring of her money, her daughter coming and going and growing older herself. But she thinks she has made a fair trade, all things considered. It is a way to live. Here, in the bright, noontime restaurant, it seems not a bad way. She has driven here in her new car; she will pay for the food; and still she sees beauty in the things she sees alone. Around them, unnoticed by anyone else, the waitresses are tracing their predictable paths among the tables. In their white shirts, under the high windows, they circle, and Andie watches them. Deft and kind, they make no false moves. It is an inviting, vigorous motion, a small thing, but she takes pleasure in it. Sitting with her aunt, she is put in mind of the old dirt road, the summer fields, and it makes her want to walk, to bustle about. Beneath the table, hidden from view, she begins to shuffle her feet, once, twice; and for a moment she almost walks in place. From other tables, Andie thinks, she may appear to be dancing.

# Blue River, Blue Sun

Joseph couldn't get anyone to buy his dead father's house, and he knew why: it was old and full of his dead father's things, and the roof leaked when it rained. But Joseph couldn't clean out the closets or mow the lawn or really do anything normal because his wife May had filed for divorce and it was just about killing him. It also took up most of his spare time, so for two months Joseph spent his days teaching and most of his evenings with his lawyer, Alan Pinkerman, in his lawyer's green-carpeted office in the mall, Joseph's weakening heart stretched on a rack while Alan Pinkerman sharpened pencils and sucked coffee back and forth through his terrible teeth. Joseph himself lived those two months in a grim yellow-walled apartment, lost a good deal of his white hair, and then in October his wife May won the divorce anyway and got what amounted to everything: their ratty condo in Bellevue and what little money they had. In the condo's tiny garage May left him his geology books and his maps and two black trash bags full of his clothes. Saddened and embarrassed, Joseph loaded his belongings into the back of his clattering van, drove to his father's house, and moved his things in, telling himself he was killing two birds with one stone.

Actually he liked his father's house; it was a big place. He shambled through its long rooms, peered into the empty refrigerator, picked up the telephone to hear the ominous dial tone. He heaved himself up the carpeted stairs and into his old boyhood bedroom, under the eaves. On this bed as a boy Joseph had imagined the long life before him, the tall women and other cities, and in summer he had slept with the window open and the boats buzzing past outside, but what had once long ago been the world was now rickety and easily seen as only one version of things. Back downstairs, he tacked his maps to the living room walls. He was a geologist; he studied rivers.

During the first week of the divorce, Joseph spent a good deal of time by himself, poking around the house and working hard at not thinking about anything. He walked up and down the stairs, stacked and restacked the firewood in the watery basement. He vacuumed often. At some point he ended up opening his father's bedroom closet, where he found the old man's shoes. His father had been a meticulous man, an alphabetizer of books, and here the round shoes were lined up like stones. Joseph crouched to examine them, turned each one over gingerly, as though he were handling a delicate jar, to examine the rubber tread; then he narrowed his hands and put them deep into a pair of loafers and clopped a few idiotic steps on all fours. Against his fingertips the dark, oily imprints of his father's toes felt as though they might have held almonds.

Hanging above the shoes were his father's fifteen powder-blue suits, like fifteen men standing obediently in the dark. They were seersucker suits, out of place in this gray city, but his father had worn them all his life, occasionally replacing one when it went too far out of fashion. Joseph took the suits from the closet one by one and laid them carefully on his father's bed, one atop the other. Together the puckered suits made a cushy stack two and a half feet thick and filled the room with a sky-blue light, turning the sickly yellow quilt to a comforting undersea green. They smelled richly of the old man, and for a moment his father was back in the room, and in a good mood. Joseph felt a calm orderliness come over him, a brief sense that all could be set right with the world. At this he gasped and began to cry, then stopped abruptly, ashamed that it was the old man's suits that had brought this on. Joseph himself wasn't at all young anymore and now he lived alone, in the house his parents had owned, envying his father's clothes. He put them back in the closet and tried to forget them.

Sometime during the second week he began to think of things he didn't want to think of. He was sad, and he missed May terribly. She was a psychologist and had left him for another psychologist, Brian Loop, the man she shared an office with, and Joseph thought of her constantly. He thought of May sleeping with Brian, both of them living a normal, well-ordered life in Joseph's old condo and May not missing Joseph a bit, and he hated it. He thought of Brian shitting in the toilet that had once muffled his own bellowing farts, and thought of Brian scratching his damp little dick in the kitchen Joseph and May had shared, and Joseph hated the man and May too, even while he missed her.

Now and then Joseph missed his father as well though the old man had lived a long life and had never deceived himself with thoughts of God or anything benign in the universe. The cardboard box of his ashes was really all the old man had come to, and the old man had understood this. Joseph, to his embarrassment, was less firm on the matter; now and then he thought hopefully of a god or some amiable basically disinterested spirit who watched things as a man might watch traffic from a bridge. In the rain and cold after Christmas Joseph scattered his father's ashes illicitly into Lake Washington, leaning over the side of a rented aluminum canoe. His father spread like dust or pollen over the rolling surface of the water, bits of bone spinning among the gray sift. That was all it came to: years of eating and worrying, and this was how you ended up, a mark on the water. Water took you away and spread you evenly around the shore of a lake, and the lake emptied into the Sound, the Sound into the ocean. There were no boats out that day, and Joseph had the wintry lake to himself. He was happy for that, at least.

During January Joseph went about his world as best he could. Unburdened by human contact, he walked through his days with as few thoughts as a dog. He went off to work every day, where Paula, the department secretary, smiled sympathetically and answered his mail. Many of the rooms in his house he rarely entered. He'd once had a brother but the brother was dead, his mother was long dead, and Joseph was the last of his line. Superstitiously he stayed away from the room where his father had died, the old man staring at the ceiling with his big brown teeth stuffing his mouth like dice. When he considered his father's strange, meticulous ways, Joseph thought he had understood him only as well as he might have understood a tree; and sometimes Joseph himself felt like a tree, with his arms extended, and light passing vaguely through him.

To his surprise, things did not improve with time. He entertained no lovers, though he had often heard of divorced men doing such things. Women took no notice of him now, he was short and not thin, most of the hair on the back of his head was gone, and what was left swirled around his face as though he had just come in from the wind. His students appreciated his attentions, but he had nowhere else to put them, and he felt he was merely doing his job. He had never listened much to the radio, had hardly watched television, so days and weeks passed in which the only sounds in the old house were those of the mice in the walls, and usually rain spitting on the windows, and Joseph's footsteps back and forth over the booming floors as he went from the bathroom to the refrigerator to the window. The house was on a hill and looked down a slope toward the lake, and at night from his bedroom Joseph could see red lights flashing here and there on the water, the same red lights that had flashed outside the window when he was a boy, except now he was inexplicably old and his wife was gone, and his father. In his dreams the red lights were those of a far shore, the land of the dead, a place it seemed he had lived in sight of all his life.

Joseph felt very old now — he felt awful — and soon he came to think he might be dying, too. In February, when the rain let up, Joseph went to the doctor, a man his own age with pink spots on his cheeks that looked like makeup. In the bright fluorescent office the doctor twisted his watch on his hairy wrist and said there was nothing wrong, that Joseph was healthy for a man his age, and that he could expect maybe twenty more years, good years, before everything went to pot, assuming, of course, there was no catastrophe down the line. Joseph slid from the plastic examining table with the sanitary paper wadded somehow between his knees, thanked the doctor, and left. It was all bad news. It had been months since he'd seen May, but he called her, and she answered on the second ring. It was the first good thing that had happened in a long while.

He waited for her at a German restaurant in the mall. Women dressed in Bavarian costumes served sausages and pancakes and poured him thin, bitter coffee. He sat at a table near the entrance and looked out at the bright concourse. He loved the mall; it was a kind of heaven. Alan Pinkerman's glass-fronted office was right across from the restaurant, and Joseph could see Juliet's square blond head staring into her computer. He hated his lawyer for many things, for the motel prints on his walls and the green monogrammed pencils he gave away, and he hated Pinkerman's pink family on the desk in their oval frames. He hated his lawyer for having lost him everything.

But he loved the mall; it was why he had chosen Pinkerman in the first place, a childishness he wouldn't have admitted to anyone. The mall comforted him, though he knew it was designed to do exactly that. Amiable stairways directed him from place to place through the ferns. Passengers in the glass elevator stood, still and serious, watching the floor of the mall come up to meet them or fall away. Fountains rose toward the skylights.

May slid into the booth across from him and for a moment Joseph stared blankly at her face, which was not quite as he remembered it. It was more moony, powdered, and there were earrings, gold and dangling, where before there had been nothing. But it was May, with her chin in the air. She put her purse on the table and said, "Hello, Joseph."

"Hello," he said.

"And how are you?"

"Fine," he said, "just fine."

She touched her powdered cheek and narrowed her eyes. "I hope you don't mind my saying you don't look terribly well."

He checked himself in the back of his spoon but saw nothing unusual. "And how are *you?*"

"Oh." She looked out into the mall. "I'm fine too."

"How's Brian?"

"Brian." She shrugged. "As far as Brian ever is just fine, Brian's just fine. He's working very hard." She was well kept, her hair pinned back, the sharp point of her chin roaming toward him, then away. "But we're doing fine."

"Good," he said, desperately. "It's good to see you."

She smiled.

"I'm glad you're happy," he said, and this was basically true. She had run out of patience with his general gloominess and had found a younger, less dreary man — there was probably more to it than that, but not much more. He couldn't honestly complain: she was nice enough to come say hello when she owed him nothing and he wasn't poor or sick, only very, very sad. "You look good." He had more to say, but he couldn't think how to begin.

"Thank you."

He turned his spoon over.

"I imagine you must miss your father," she said, and fingered her necklace.

"I scattered him. Threw him out in Lake Washington."

She lifted her eyebrows. "Really? I was worried you'd keep him around on the mantel."

"No."

"You always did linger over things. That house, for example."

"I'm living there now."

"Yes, I know." She sighed. "I think it's a mistake."

"Why?"

"Oh, Joseph." She gave him a pitying smile. "You ask why."

"I like it there."

"Yes," she said, significantly. "I know you do."

"I don't know what you mean by that."

She shrugged and looked away, maneuvering her wire bracelet.

He cleared his throat. He had something to say, a hopeless thing. He debated for a moment about saying it, and then he said it. "I miss you," he said.

"Oh, Joseph, please. None of that," she said, softly. She lifted her purse and stood up.

"Wait. I didn't mean it. I was joking."

"No, no, no." She spoke quietly, her head down. "You can't imagine what I had to do to get here today." She opened her purse and closed it, then looked at him severely. "How about this, Joseph? Let's make an agreement. From now on I give you my permission to pretend I'm dead, too. Just dead and gone. I think it might do you some good. All right?"

People were watching from the other booths. He said, "May."

She shook her head once. "No, Joseph." She put her purse over her shoulder and walked into the mall, where she vanished.

*　　*　　*

In this mood it was unsafe to think of his good days with May, but he couldn't help himself. One year early in their marriage she'd worked as a radio psychologist, nine to midnight, and in those days he had listened to her as he walked around their little apartment, and later, too, as he lay in bed, not out of any erotic longing, but enjoying her presence, such as it was; and as he drifted off, her smooth voice had created a sort of island, to which he would cling for a moment at the edge of sleep, then let go. And in the morning, there she would be, beside him, like magic, as though he had dreamed her to life. People had turned to hear her voice in restaurants. How beautiful her throat, her sharp chin. So much, so many of his days, had been hers.

Months passed. At the university Joseph faced his classes with confusion. The students had become suddenly younger, but at the same time they were very worldly, addressing him as Joseph and interrupting when he spoke. He didn't mind, he decided, and secretly he liked being addressed as an equal. But when he saw his students traipsing across campus in their bright colors and complicated backpacks, he was vaguely ashamed of himself, his ratty clothes, his six pairs of corduroy pants endlessly circulated. When May was with him he had owned some dignity, though now it seemed it had merely been on loan. For years he had gone about this life, paying little attention to anything, but with May around it hadn't mattered. His life had meant something with May; it had been a legitimate enterprise. Now he had nothing to show for anything. No old students ever called him up and took him out for coffee, he loved his maps and rivers but where did they get him? He knew gallons per second, he knew fish populations and die rates and all of it, but it made no difference, he was alone. His hair grew longer and longer. He needed new shoes. He gave out grades in the old perfunctory way, leaning hard into the bubble sheet with his dull lead pencil.

The summer went by, cool and pleasant, and it was September again. The sky hung sullen under endless clouds. The rivers he studied became clotted with mud, and he slogged through cold marshes and estuaries without energy. The plastic water vials shifted in his pack like tiny men shifting in sleep, and when he dipped to fill a sample his old knees popped and pinged. Away across the grasses he could see his students advancing one slow step at a time. In the truck going home the students laughed and wrote in their notebooks while he listened to the sloshing in the trunk and felt the steering wheel like a bone beneath his fingers. Every morning the gray city rose in the bedroom window as though it were a thousand years old and unchangeable.

In October, when it suddenly grew warm, Joseph found he had trouble opening his bedroom window, which had swelled with the September rain. He grasped the brass handles and pulled upward with all his strength. He felt something pop, then a strange slithering in his gut, and a tearing pain. With one hand on his belly he drove himself to the hospital, where he was told he had a hernia. He called and left a message on May's machine, saying he was going into surgery. Riding on his back into the prep room Joseph watched the hallway lights pass over his head, one after the other, and as the mask was fitted to his face he found himself with May when they were both young. Before he fell asleep he saw her young body at the river's edge, but when he woke, he was alone. He wondered where May was and realized he had never thought of her not coming. Down the hall he could hear a woman singing, but it was no one he knew. There was a whirring sound behind his right shoulder, but in his pain he couldn't turn to see what it was and had to wait an hour before the nurse, in her crackling whites, told him it was an air conditioner. When she reached up to turn it off Joseph saw the smooth lunule of her armpit and recognized that it was the first time in almost exactly a year he'd really looked at a woman. It was, to his surprise, a nice moment, as though something had been sealed off and settled. To the nurse he said, "And a very pleasant good morning to you."

"It's midnight," she said, giving him a shot.

"You don't say."

"Oh, but I do," she said, and left the room.

"Okay," said Joseph, and turned on the television. Despite the shot he was up all night, listening to the bonging in the corridors, and when he checked out the next afternoon, happy in his old clothes, and made his way across the asphalt parking lot to his solitary van, he felt, for no reason he could understand, as though he could walk for weeks.

*　　*　　*

It was a funny time of year: October, becoming November, usually a season of strong effects but this year mild and uneventful, clouds puttering over the city and moving off again over the mountains. Halloween night he spent on a chair in the front hall, a bowl of Reese's Pieces on his lap, waiting, but no one came to the door. Lying in bed he heard tires squealing and a gale of adolescent laughter, but the next morning, a Saturday, the neighborhood was undamaged. Later that day he found himself walking the aisles of Albertson's pushing an empty cart, not knowing exactly what he wanted; eventually he stopped in front of the cat food, charmed by the cats on the bags. Two orange ones and a gray looked him over, the gray with her paw in the air. They were lovely things, he thought, our feline friends. How lonely he was! A woman, thirty, blond, with a baby in the cart seat, eyed him carefully. "New cat?" she asked.

"Well," he said, "in a manner of speaking."

"Here." She handed him a white bag, elegant, covered with fine print, with only a black-and-white pen drawing of a cat, artfully done. It was not his favorite. "This is *especially* good for them."

"Thank you." He looked at her baby. "You're married, I guess."

"Oh, yes," she said. "And this is Richard."

"Hello, Richard."

"Goodbye," she said, and wheeled off. "Good luck."

Disappointed, he steered around and around. His abdomen ached, and when he was alone or unobserved he slipped his fingers through his shirt and touched the hard ridge of scar above his navel. After a while he put the cat food back on the shelf and left with a carton of ice cream, and that night, while watching television, he stirred the Reese's Pieces into it. In the hospital he had discovered the real-life cop shows, and now he looked forward to them all day. I, he nodded, am not a criminal. I have no cocaine in my hat, no gun in my car. I am not a wanted man. Put this way it was a heartening thought. The days passed like this, first one, then another, but better than before.

Pain is a noise we can become accustomed to, Joseph thought as December arrived, and when it begins to ease, there may be strange effects. The woman at last out of debt wanders the aisles without desire, leaves, finds it has begun to rain, and stands under an awning for an hour. Our parents are happily reunited, and the ceiling shadows no longer hold wagons and scythes but only leaves and branches, and the sounds from the window are not mysterious postings from the larger world, merely the mailman dropping his bag. And he too, he thought, sitting in his office at the university, with the sun hanging like a rose over the library, sensed a momentary ordinariness come over him; pigeons scrabbled with their steel toes on the gutter, and he was happy. It was a jarring instant of naked relief, but just as quickly, as though in defense, he thought of May, with her little black shoes up on her desk, talking on the telephone, and at once the friendly, familiar gloom descended again. It was noon, and the cool halls were empty. He finished the last of his morning coffee, cold as stone.

It was then that Paula Hubberton, the department secretary, began walking by his open door — three times she passed in her low heels, glancing in hesitantly each time, knocking at last. She was a tall woman with brown hair and a round, open face like a dinner plate, and she leaned against the doorjamb with her long legs crossed and her arms folded across her chest. She looked arranged there, Joseph thought, and he imagined her practicing the pose at night, a cruel thought, but he had done that sort of thing himself, many years ago, when such things had mattered. She was separated or divorced, he knew that much.

"Misery loves company?"

"Sure," he said.

She sat down across from him in the green chair he kept for students. With a professional flair she swiveled in the seat, pushed the door closed with her fingertips, and took a pack of cigarettes from her shirt pocket. She offered the pack across the table, and Joseph took one.

"It's rotten," she said, blowing smoke.

He had nothing to use as an ashtray, so he put his coffee cup on the far edge of the desk. "Rotten?"

"This whole thing you've been going through with May."

"Oh, well," he said. "Wasn't much fun." He coughed, dizzy from the smoke. He wished he could think of something better to say, anything at all, but he felt incapable of conversation. When was the last real conversation he'd had? He couldn't remember. At last he said, "I guess she knew what she was doing."

"Oh, Joe, don't say that. That's pathetic. Really it is."

"Well," he said, backtracking, "okay. I guess I just mean she never really looked back."

"Ha. I don't know if I've ever told you about my husband."

"No, I don't think you have." But he couldn't remember having talked to her about anything. Far off to the west rainclouds were piling themselves against the Olympics, like gray balloons against a ceiling. But — here was a woman. She extended her long legs across his office floor. They were beautiful legs, in brown hose. He said, "Tell me."

"Oh, I'm sure you know the way these things happen. Rick suddenly gets interested in skiing, and he's never been interested in skiing before."

"Uh-oh."

"Sure. A danger signal. But I think, Well, this is fine. It's a hobby. And he buys all this equipment and spends all his time in the basement waxing it or whatever it is you do, and he buys one of those exercise machines, you know, so he goes back and forth, back and forth." She pumped her arms so her gold necklace tossed. "And I mean I'm not all that interested in skiing — seems to me a waste of time — but if he wants to do it, that's fine with me. I mean, he's a carpenter, so it's not like he doesn't spend enough time outside, but whatever."

Reflected light made watery patterns on his walls. Away across the campus a bell was tolling two, a high, beautiful sound. Things — he couldn't help it — were improving. "Go on," he said.

"Well, so he goes off to this ski class and he meets somebody, or maybe he'd met her before and they decided to go skiing as an alibi; I don't know. And this goes on for a couple of months or so until I finally take a good close look at the phone bill and it's got all these long-distance calls to Enumclaw and I'm thinking, Who do I know in Enumclaw? Nobody." She sniffed and frowned. "So I say, So Rick, who's in Enumclaw? And he says, Nobody."

"Nobody."

"Right, nobody. So I take down the number and one day I'm here at work and I decide, All right, enough is enough. I call the number."

Joseph sat motionless. May had been sleeping with Brian Loop for six months before telling him, a day Joseph counted as the worst of his life, not least because Brian Loop had seemed so harmless: he was short and had a beard and counseled a lot of local newscasters; he'd set himself up as a specialist in media stress, and in the waiting room Joseph had run into two or three people he recognized from television. Brian accompanied them to the door of his office, holding their famous shoulders. A big goofy smile. Harmless.

"So," Paula said, "I call the number and naturally it's an answering machine. But it's this little baby voice, you know? Like one of those women with baby voices?"

"Sure."

"So I say, This is Rick's wife, blah blah blah, I'd like to speak to you sometime, and about ten minutes later I get this phone call." Paula leaned forward and licked her lips. "I hope you don't mind me telling you all this."

"No."

"I just thought you'd like to know."

"Yes, tell me."

"Well, so it's her. She plays it all innocent and says, Well, I don't know anybody named Rick, never heard of him, blah blah blah. Through this whole thing, you know, she sounds like she's nine years old, and I'm thinking, Is this woman old enough to have her own phone? But eventually she kind of rears back and says, Maybe he wants something a little more exciting than you."

"Oh, boy," he said.

"I know." Paula stared at him angrily. "So that clinched it for me. And Rick tried to play dumb, too — he just kept denying it and denying it — and I said, Well, choose, then. Just choose. And he kind of looked at me and you could tell he was weighing it in his head."

"Right."

"You know how that is? I mean, you could see him imagining her tits and ass or whatever and thinking, like, What does that equal? So I said, Forget it." She drew one last time on her cigarette and tipped it into the cup. "So that's my story."

"What happened to him? He marry her?"

"He moved in with her," Paula said. "If that's what he wants, that's what he wants."

"He's happy?"

"I don't know. Probably. As far as that goes."

"Happy." His mouth tasted ashy from the cigarette. "May's happy."

"See? They leave and they don't look back. We sit and wait and wait and they don't, *don't*, look back. Gone. They're gone. We're the suckers."

"Not always."

"Always, Joe. Suckers."

"Sometimes they come back," he said, and knew at once it wasn't true.

"Joe," she said. "Think for a minute."

"All right."

"You're how old?"

"Fifty-six."

"You think May's dreaming about you?"

"Probably not."

"Exactly. My husband wanted two big tits and an exercise partner, so off he goes. I mean *fuck* it, Joe. They just don't deserve any happiness in their lives."

"Yeah."

"They don't."

"Maybe not," he said. But they did. Everybody did.

"Your wife's a psychiatrist?"

"Psychologist."

"Well, she sounds pretty fucked up to me."

"Maybe so," he said.

She said, "How'd you like to have a drink sometime?"

He said, "Of course I would." This was a date, he thought, a little alarmed. "Yes, I'd like that. I don't get out much anymore."

"Tonight?" She cleared her throat and looked at him seriously.

He thought of his cluttered house, the maps draped over everything. "No," he said, "let's make it tomorrow." Later, driving home, he thought about this phrase and felt uneasy, but only briefly.

Pleased with himself, he decided to drive to the mall. He went to Nordstrom's and bought a pack of blue underwear; then, swinging the bag against his knee, he went into Foot Locker and bought a pack of white cushy socks, guaranteed for life against holes. He saw a pair of sunglasses in The Accessory Lady which made him look all right, so he bought them, though he was the only man in the store and suspected they might be women's sunglasses. He couldn't bring himself to buy a shirt — the nice ones were all at least forty dollars — and pants were out of the question, but he was happy with his haul and went off toward the German restaurant. On his way, he decided to visit his lawyer, Alan Pinkerman.

"You're back," Pinkerman said behind his glass desk. His long brown hair curled over his collar. He was in his thirties, Joseph guessed, and skinny like a stray dog.

"I was in the neighborhood. Thought I'd say hello."

"Yeah. Good." Pinkerman puffed his cheeks. "Something I can do for you?"

"No, no," Joseph said. He had really meant nothing by the visit, or so he thought, but now he had a peculiar attraction to Pinkerman; he wanted to pinch a fingerful of his coarse hair, to examine the wide sloppy knot of his tie. "How's things?" he asked.

"Oh, things are fucked up. As usual. Let's get something to eat. I'm doing nothing here."

They walked out into the burbling mall. Women pushed babies in their strollers. Teenage girls strutted in their preposterous mascara. Joseph had lost all his friends when May left, and suddenly he felt that loss again; they had gravitated toward the more glamorous, the more interesting of the pair, and May was that.

"I love this place," Joseph said.

Pinkerman jingled his keys. "You're supposed to love it."

They walked along in silence, past SallyAnn's, Mrs. Fields, The Bon, past Eddie Bauer and the Cockatoo Corner, where a hundred birds hopped and sang, tilting their heads. Somewhere he could hear water running. They stood in line for pizza.

"I haven't had pizza in months," Joseph said.

"Maybe you need to get out a little more."

"Oh, I do," Joseph said, "I do."

Pinkerman picked up their slices and carried them to one of the plastic tables. Joseph followed.

"Believe it or not," Pinkerman said, spreading his napkin over his lap, "I know what you're here for. This happens a lot. Guys come looking for an explanation of what happened to them." Pinkerman lunged at his food.

"Well, not really. I just felt like saying hello. I was buying clothes."

"Okay. There's usually an easy explanation," Pinkerman said, chewing. "So here it is. The easy explanation in your case is that you weren't what she wanted and that's that. There's no easy way to say it, but it's the easy explanation. Whatever the reasons, she didn't want you. You're sort of a Gloomy Gus, but whatever, the reasons are for you to figure out."

Joseph began eating.

"But there's usually a harder explanation, too, which is also true, but harder to get your brain around. Like maybe you two never honestly talked about what was wrong. Okay, maybe. But why not? What was it about you or her that made you two avoid talking about anything? Okay, maybe she thought everything she'd ever do in life would be a success, you know, and here she is, and she can't even keep a marriage together. That's upsetting."

"It is."

"Okay, so there's part of your explanation."

Joseph nodded.

"But who cares? You could go on forever with this stuff. You can explain and explain and think about it every day until you die. I get people I divorced ages ago coming back to me, taking me out for coffee. They haven't seen their wives in eight, ten years, and I'm the closest they can get. I mean, I get a *lot* of guys who come in like this and they say, Jesus Christ, I can't just *start over,* you know? There's no break in anything, I mean all I did was go to sleep and wake up and go to sleep and wake up a bunch of times and I got old, look at me, I'm an old man and all I did was live my life, how's that supposed to happen? Those are the guys you worry about. Obviously, obviously, obviously, it's not worth it."

"I've spent a lot of time thinking about her."

"Well, you should, right? Sure you should. It's a big thing in your life. But there's a limit. Sooner or later you move on. Usually the sooner the better."

"I think things are getting better. And there's this other woman," he said. The plastic bags rested like two big cats against his leg.

"Great. That's the ticket. If the opportunity presents itself and you feel all right about it, then by all means go ahead. You don't have to honor anything anymore. You can start over. That's one of the few good things about a situation like this. But it's a trick of the mind. It's double-think. You have to know what you're doing and at the same time pay no attention to whatever weird stuff comes up when you're with a new woman, if you know what I mean."

Joseph felt a great bubble rising in him: it was a sigh, and it lasted a long while.

"Jesus," Pinkerman said. "It's all right."

"I don't know."

"One thing a lot of the guys I see have in common? They pretend it's not there. Whatever it is. If they ignore it, it'll go away. It doesn't. Like death. It does not go away. And by the time they see me, it's too late. I'm the doctor, I say make yourself comfortable, see all your friends again. But forget it. But you? You know it's there. You're okay. You're alive. So go do something with your life. That's all you can do." Pinkerman wiped his mouth with finality and crumpled his napkin into a tiny hard ball. "That's all I can say."

When Joseph woke the next morning, the low clouds hung in the treetops. He was cold, and his knees popped audibly as he made his way to the bathroom, where he examined himself skeptically in the mirror. He trimmed his unruly eyebrows, little hairs settling to the bottom of the sink. Then he shaved with great care, scraping his old gray sail of a face until it was pink and raw. In the shower he soaped and cupped his stringy balls in one hand; they too had become absurdly hairy, and he wondered whether he ought to do something about it, though he couldn't imagine what, exactly. Things were running more or less to seed. But he liked his body, his simple physical self, and when he toweled off he examined with some affection the familiar patterns of hair on his arms, the deep liquid droop of his belly, his scar. It was the only thing that was keeping him from the void, after all, an alarming thought that he quickly put out of mind.

He dressed in his new underwear and socks and picked a white shirt from the back of his bedroom chair. Then he went to his father's bedroom, opened the closet, and took one of the blue suits from the rod. It held the rich, damp smell of most closets and still, faintly, that old narrow bright smell that had been his father's. It looked as good as the day it was made, and it pleased him to think of the old man taking such good care of things. The sleeves fit snugly over his upper arms. The fabric gathered and puckered in all the right places, and Joseph looked like a gentleman in it. He admired himself in the mirror and set about straightening up the house.

That afternoon he met Paula at a bar near the campus. They sat at a high table by the window, which made Joseph a little uncomfortable; he felt as though he were on display in his new suit. Buses swished through the rain, their interiors lit. Paula, her hands palms up on the table, said, "You hear from her much anymore?"

"May? No," Joseph said, "but my lawyer thinks I should move on."

"Move on. That's right. Move on. It's time." She examined her hands, which looked swollen, as if slightly overinflated.

"Some weather we're having," he said.

"So Rick was all into that kind of extra-rationalist thinking, you know? He'd wake up and tell me about his dreams, and finally I just said, Why don't you start writing those things down? But he never did."

Joseph cautiously moved his hand across the table and touched one of her palms with his fingertips. The skin was taut, dry. She took his hand and went on, calmly examining it. "The man never believed in cause and effect to begin with, that was the main thing. He'd come home and tell me there was this big cloud that went over at work shaped like his head, like this big Rick head, and then he got a headache. Honestly. I'm not making this up."

"You wouldn't make anything up," he said.

"I make things up all the time," she said. "If there's a point I'm trying to make. Or if I have an ulterior purpose, if you know what I mean." She flicked her eyebrows up and down.

"I didn't mean that."

"You were flirting with me for a second," she said.

"Sorry."

"No, it's good," she said. "Rick never flirted. After a while, anyway. Then, *pssht,* off he goes."

"You know about May."

She shrugged, kindly. "Sure."

The bar clattered around them. Suddenly he remembered the red lights bobbing in the harbor and felt the old sadness creeping on again. He hadn't meant to let it happen this time. He'd wanted to be happy, but he felt as though he'd just stepped in a hole. "God," he said. "May."

"Joe," she said, "don't do this."

"I can't help it."

"Sucker," she said. "Don't be a sucker."

The rain had grown heavier, and they both watched it for a moment. This was the time, he thought; if he was to do it, he'd do it now. Double-think, he thought, and tried to force the idea from his mind. He said, "Why don't we take a little drive?"

"Good idea." She put her cigarettes back in her purse. Her hands, he saw, were shaking. He paid for their drinks, took two mints from the glass dish at the register, and walked with her, bravely, he thought, into the rain.

In the car he kissed her. She seemed surprised and gave a little cry, but kissed him back. Her lips were soft; he had forgotten how good it felt to kiss someone. They were parked on a street of shabby student houses. Orange couches sat on lopsided porches. Paula's small, swollen hand went to his thigh and squeezed. "Not here."

"No." He started the car.

He drove across the University Bridge, the metal grate of the bridge deck humming under the tires. He drove south, up the side of Capitol Hill, down Broadway. Her hand sat on his leg, occasionally squeezing, and once he reached over and felt her knee, rounded and soft under the fabric of her pants. She smelled of cigarettes and wet clothes.

"Turn left here," she said.

They went down a street of brick apartment buildings and small wooden houses. Paula peered out the window, her hand still on his leg. "This is it," she said. It was an apartment building like any other, four stories tall with an awning.

He stopped the car. He had an idea where they were. "Your husband's place?" he said.

She sat looking up at a high window. "I saw her coming out of here once." She sniffed, and Joseph wondered whether she was crying. "Your wife's with someone else, right?"

"Guy named Brian."

"They live together?"

"Yeah."

She turned to him, angrily. "Why do they do this?" Her eyes were red and her hair had fallen across her face.

"Wait a minute," he said.

"Now I'm whining," she said. "But I can do that."

"Sure." He pushed her hair out of her eyes. "You can whine if you want."

She undid her seatbelt and got out of the car. She jogged across the rainy street, her long legs scissoring in her dark jeans. She stopped under the awning. She rang the buzzer, leaning into it.

Joseph watched.

She waited a second, then sprinted back to the car.

"Forget it," she said, gasping, her hair slicked around her face. "This is stupid. This isn't all I talk about, by the way, I know it seems like it but it's not. This is just a little relapse." She waved her hands in front of her. "Forget it." Beside him in the car she sighed once, deeply.

Joseph reached into the breast pocket of the blue suit jacket and handed her one of the mints. "Thanks," she said.

"Want to go back to my place?"

"No." She tore at the plastic wrapper. "Just keep driving."

So they drove around the rainy city, up and down the teetering hills, through the Arboretum, under the dripping trees. It was dark, though only three in the afternoon, and everyone had their headlights on. From the top of Queen Anne they rounded a curve, where they could see the Sound. Tankers sat at anchor in the harbor, and long white ferries headed across the water, turning like compass needles toward Bremerton. Paula rested her chin on her palm and stared through the windshield. Occasionally she rolled her forehead around on her window.

"Don't think about it," he said. "It doesn't help."

"You know, I'd kill him if I thought I could get away with it. I really would. I'd split his fucking skull open. Or you, I watch you mope around like that for a year. May would not last long in an alley with *moi*, I can tell you."

"She's pretty tough."

"Rip her fucking throat out, Joe. What she did to you."

He didn't know what he was supposed to say to that, but he didn't think it mattered. He found his way to the freeway and drove across

Lake Washington, the bridge almost empty this early in the afternoon, and then he kept driving, heading east out of the city. He drove through the smooth, concrete suburbs on the East Side without looking twice, the thousands of identical houses marching up and down what he had once known as forested hills. He drove through Issaquah and up into the mountains.

He had no destination in mind until they passed over Snoqualmie and left the clouds behind. On this side of the mountains the sun was strong, the day almost warm. He saw the ski lifts swinging, the winter lodges bare and exposed in the wintry mountain sunlight, and all of a sudden he knew where he wanted to go. He turned off the freeway and drove through Cle Elum and over a small metal bridge.

"God, the sun," Paula said, turning her face to it like a cat. "Imagine that."

Joseph put on his new sunglasses.

He turned onto a smaller road, then a smaller one, this one unpaved. Feeling brave and peculiar, he crossed another bridge and pulled the car onto the ragged shoulder.

"This is the Teanaway River." He gestured over his shoulder. "Down there."

She nodded, businesslike. "Okay."

They got out of the car. Trees on both sides of the road grew tall toward a blue sky. Joseph in his blue suit was warm and happily contained. He rolled his shoulders and felt the fabric creak and stretch. Paula in her tennis shoes followed him across the road and back toward the bridge. He had never been here before, but he found a path down the riverbank and over stones to the water's edge. The river was shallow, four feet of clear water.

Paula took off her shoes and socks and rolled up the cuffs of her jeans. "Jesus Christ," she said, dipping her feet in. "That's cold."

Joseph did the same, enjoying the trustworthy feel of the fabric as it bunched against his calves. He sat beside her, his legs dangling in the water.

"Aren't you cold?" she asked.

"Well, I guess I am." But he stood up in the sun, shaking his wet feet, and took off his suit jacket and spread it carefully on a broad rock. Then he pulled out his shirttail and unbuttoned and removed his white shirt. His gut hung over his belt.

"Pardon my gut," he said, sitting down. "An old man's belly."

"I like it." She palmed it and squeezed.

He leaned back. "Look at this. Hernia." He ran his forefinger along it. "Ugly old thing." The scar ran horizontally over his stomach, as long as a crayon and almost as hard.

She reached to touch it.

"I was trying to open a window."

She slid her hand into his crotch and moved closer to him. "You're not so old."

"I know," he said. "Neither are you."

She kissed him and began undoing his belt. "There's nobody around."

"No."

"Please tell me the cold won't affect you," she said.

"I don't think so."

"Then take off your clothes," she said, and in a moment they were both naked. Paula's breasts were very small and round, like scoops of ice cream. She rubbed her arms. "Cold," she said.

Naked, Joseph wanted to be clothed, or at least covered, so he stepped into the river. It was colder than seemed possible, a river of ice, but he tried to ignore it, his big feet moving clumsily from stone to stone until he reached the deeper water and sandy bottom, where he could crouch and hide himself. Paula followed, laughing. Her expression was full of happy desperation, her eyebrows high on her forehead, her little breasts wiggling as she leaped toward him.

She fell against him in the middle of the river. Here they crouched together and began kissing again. It had been long, so long, since he'd had sex, but he hadn't forgotten anything. The river was killingly cold, but she was up and down on him with vigor, splashing and once slipping off. He heard their voices coming back to them from the riverbanks. It was wonderful sex; he had missed sex like this.

When they were finished she kissed his neck and put her nose in his ear. "Very, *very* good," she said. "Solidarity forever."

"Thank you."

"No, thank *you*," she said. "I think I'm getting hypothermia."

"Paula," he said.

They crouched in the river a minute more, watching the water ripple under the bridge.

"I'm *really* getting cold," she said.

"Paula," he said again. "This is a good day."

"Good." She waded toward the shore, pink all over. "I think I have no toes."

"I mean it," he said. "A good day." He squinted at the sun. He lifted his feet from the sand and began floating down the river, naked, on his back, letting the water take him. It was a slow river, and quiet. Above him, Joseph saw the blue sky piping away through the banks of trees; he saw the sun hanging over the rim of the mountains. To Joseph it seemed he had stepped into the air and was looking down from a great height on a new river no one had ever entered, a narrow river of sky, a place where the air and the sun were both blue, in a new country no one had ever seen. Birds drifted over the surface of this new river, tipping their wings. He spread his arms in the enveloping water. Upstream, near the bridge, the empty blue suit assumed its simple human shape on the rock.

# Wizard

Y OU COULD TELL the Players Theater in Eugene had been a
glamorous place in its prime, maybe back in the thirties —
the chandeliers still spun in the lobby, and the big ornate
balcony still swept across the back of the hall — but somewhere along
the line things had gone sour, the neighborhood had gone to hell, and
when I got there we couldn't light the furnace except during perform-
ances, and the red velvet seats were torn and patched — we took turns
sewing them — and the water in the toilets, when there was any, was
always rusty. Across the street was a big Ryder rental yard and a liquor
store, and people crept around in the parking lot at night and set off
car alarms. But I enjoyed being there: I liked the cold and the penury,
taking them as signs of our virtue and cultivation, and I loved the
back crannies, too, the deep basement prop rooms where the old
painted stage sets leaned against the walls like ruins, the cardboard
bricks light as air when you bent to move them. You got the sense that
you were doing something dutiful and kind, putting on plays, giving
people a good time — and you had to feel that way; there wasn't any
money in it. One way or another all of us wanted a better life, but the
whole thing wasn't bad, as a stopgap.

I did what you'd call assistant directing, probably, but really I did
whatever needed doing: I worked as a lighting man for a while, climbing around in the rafters with my leather gloves. Above me the ceiling
opened and opened, forty feet at least of darkness, into which I could

see the shapes of ladders and ropes disappearing, and if I climbed up toward the ceiling I could hear the rain hammering on the old tile roof and running down the gutters into the alley. Often we had a certain amount of smoke to contend with during rehearsals, especially if the play called for gunshots, so by the third act we'd get a big rolling smoke cloud collected up there above the stage, wispy, moving with mysterious grace, extending a long limb hesitantly, then pulling it back again, as though it were mulling something over. I could watch it for hours, and often it was a lot more interesting than what was on stage: two chairs, a man in black, a woman playing Death for a change. It was that sort of theater.

I'd been working on a play about Thomas Edison for a long time, a thing I started in college and kept banging away on, and one summer around this time I finished it; in the fall season, after a little wrangling, we produced it. A week into the casting a guy named Howard Turner walked in holding his raincoat over his arm, looking curiously around the theater as though he were thinking of buying the place. He was a high school chemistry teacher, forty years old, and he read more or less naturally, leaning to one side with his hand on his belly, his eyebrows lifting now and then as he stood in the yellow light. He had a big black smudge on his white shirt, and he was tall and a little fat, and his hair was matted and greasy around his hatline. We signed him up.

We rehearsed four nights a week for six weeks or so, and sometimes when rehearsals were over Turner pulled on his black raincoat and shambled with me down the street to a shitty little tavern where he played Pik-A-Winner scratch cards and drank Henry Weinhard's from the bottle. He shelled peanuts with one hand and farted by leaning to one side. "The one-cheek sneak," he said, grinning across the table. I wasn't much of a drinker, but I put on appearances, in part because drinking with him made me feel older, or, I guess, made me feel as though I were in a more advanced state of decline, which is how age appeared to me then. We were there, ostensibly, to work out the few remaining kinks in the script, but we never looked at it — we just drank — and Turner talked, accepting me generously as a peer, though I was far younger and had to strain to appear tired of the workings of life. "You divorced?" he asked me. I was twenty-six.

"Do I look divorced?"

"Married?"

"No."

He turned his bottle, peering at it. "What, gay?"

"No, just single."

"What do you think of Janine?"

"She's nice," I said.

"She's a good-looking woman. Wouldn't mind expanding my role a little bit."

"I bet you wouldn't," I said. Janine Richardson played Mary Stilwell, Edison's wife.

"A little nudie scene'd be nice," he said.

"Fifty bucks and I'll think about it."

Turner said, "You know the story about her ex-husband?" He shifted his big ass in his chair. "Guy named Ray Lunk, worked for the school district. Years ago, before your time. He was one dumb fuck." He scratched a card with a nickel and, after examining it momentarily, threw it to the floor. "Skimmed some money off the school district and bought himself a Cadillac, this big old gigantic white car, used to see him driving it around town. They nailed him for embezzlement and she divorced him. A big story around here."

"No kidding."

Turner played a few more cards, throwing them all away. Then he said, "But you know, I don't think she was totally happy about it. I think she had some mixed feelings."

"About the divorce?"

"Yeah. You notice she won't talk to me off stage."

"I noticed that."

"I think she associates me with her past. Those public school days. She sees me, she sees Ray Lunk. I guess I make her feel bad."

"Makes sense to me," I said.

"I guess it does." He sighed and put his bottle down on the script. "Just one naked scene would really mean a lot to me."

"She'd kick my ass."

He smirked. "I bet she would."

"Fuck you."

He held up his hands. "All right," he said. "Never mind."

*　　*　　*

Janine Richardson, the woman playing Mary Stilwell, was a drama
teacher from the University of Oregon. In her bursting leather satchel
she carried little dialogues written by her students:

> A (pleedingly): Take me away from here.
> B (happily): Oh, yes, my darling, this is why I
>    came to your house today.
> A: You are my sole mate.

She was maybe in her middle thirties, though of course I never
asked, and she looked a little like Mary Stilwell, with her long dark
hair and broad, pretty face. I told her this once and she rolled her eyes,
so I learned not to compliment her. We saw in each other a kindred
cynicism, or, maybe closer to the truth, I wished I were as cynical as
she, so I admired her. She wore black turtlenecks and tight black jeans,
and from the depths of her satchel she took lipstick and gum and her
cigarettes, all of them linty and damaged. We went out for coffee a few
times after rehearsal, and in the bright student café I saw the wiggly
red threads in her eyes and the pink tinge around the rims of her
nostrils. I didn't ask her about Ray Lunk or his long white car; I was
afraid to. She ordered coffee and no food, and she watched me eat my
french fries, one after the other. She smoked constantly. She had no
children and didn't want them. "Kids give me the *willies*," she said.
Her voice was husky. "I guess you're nuts about them. Teacher."

"It's just a job." I was a substitute teacher. "And besides, what are
you?"

"Teaching college is different," she said. "Most of the time."

"I see."

"But *that* must be the worst job in the world. Substitute." She
peered at me, blowing smoke to the side. "The kids ever hit you?"

"No," I said. "They usually don't pay me any attention at all."

"Ever fear for your life?"

"No. They're just kids."

"It must be very rewarding," she said.

"It is, sometimes," I said. And then, venturing, I said, "But most of
them are dummies."

"Oh, don't," she said. "You're too young to talk that way. It's ugly."

I didn't say anything.

"It's their fucking parents' fault," she said, sullenly. "Turn on the tube and go out boozing, come home and beat each other up."

"Yeah."

"Now *I* can talk that way," she said, scowling. "But I'm an old lady."

I wanted to invite her back to my place, but I had the idea that if she came home with me I'd speak her name rapturously, or I'd look secretly at her with love and get caught — that somehow I'd end up showing her how uncynical and hopeful I really was, and she would despise me for it or think me too young and innocent, unsuitable. This was all stupid, it turned out, but in the beginning I didn't know much about her or what she might find attractive. I wanted to tell her about Mary Stilwell's young curls, and her final brutal fever, but I was afraid I'd speak of Mary with too much love, and Janine would become suspicious. "What the hell *is* this place? Whose *books* are these?" she might say, stepping critically through my house, her arms folded. We always ended up walking the rainy nighttime streets of Eugene, I back to my car, she to hers.

But she played her part well, as far as I could judge such things, and it was gratifying to see Mary Stilwell walking around in the lights, speaking as I had imagined her speaking. Before she married Edison she'd worked in his laboratory, just another girl doing the usual dreary work, but her letters, written in her tiny, intelligent hand, show she liked being there. A certain glamour attached itself to anything having to do with Edison; even then he was famous for his new kind of magic, for conjuring voices from a silver cylinder, and in various circles the phonograph was thought to be a literal miracle, the herald of a coming miraculous age — and what, really, is this day but that? It's easy to see what they meant, anyway.

So Mary caught glimpses of Edison as he careened through rooms, smoky and rumpled, his knuckles big as walnuts. He smoothed his awful hair with his great hand, he screamed at people, he rammed his fists into the walls, he popped buttons off his vest, he disappeared for days. From somewhere in the building came mysterious bangs and booms, never explained. Like all the girls, Mary was suspicious of the big magnetized dynamo in the corner, which pulled out her hairpins and tugged at her buttons, playing at undressing her. Strange acrid fogs drifted through the lab, burning her eyes. In a letter to her sister she described Edison's filthy hands and sculpted hair and the gloomy shadows like hammocks under his eyes, but we are also given to understand that she was drawn to the man's power and mystery, and who wouldn't have been? She must have imagined certain scenarios — the late night alone in the laboratory, the darkened room, the smoky sky outside, the hand on her cheek — mild thoughts to keep herself entertained.

Then, and we don't know why, exactly, Edison began to court her. In the laboratory he appeared behind her, smelly and unkempt, while she punched holes in telegraph tape, her stubby fingers depressing one mechanical key after another. They walked the fields together; they drove carriages through the countryside. When he proposed to her, by a pond, she looked down at her folded hands, in a demure gesture common to the times. During their engagement he taught her Morse code, and when they were together in company he spoke to her secretly by tapping a coin on her palm.

The play ended, more or less, when Mary died of typhoid in the summer of 1884. In thirteen years she'd had three children, and Edison had to wake them all in the night and tell them their mother was dead. The biographies reveal no great history of feeling for her, at least after the marriage, but he is described as shaking and crying at her death; he could hardly talk. We can imagine him wandering through the wide halls of his house in Menlo Park, sad and disoriented, coming as if by accident to his children's bedroom doors. Do they hear him approach? The shuffle of his feet, his sobs? Some nights in that cold, empty theater, I know, I imagined him coming up the carpeted aisle in his black boots, stepping heavily, mourning, inexorable in his approach, hoping somehow things would return, magically, to their rational course.

It wasn't all I did. I taught, too, earning enough money to eat and buy my gasoline. One day I ended up at Lewis and Clark High School, where Howard Turner, as it happened, had the classroom across the hall. Early in the morning he looked unexpectedly neat — shirt pressed, hair slicked. He unlocked his door carrying a plastic coffee mug. There was a bright sparkle in his eye. "Fancy meeting you," he said.

"Back me up," I said. "I'm sending my evildoers across the hall."

But it was an uneventful day. I passed out the Dittos, and the students filled them out uncomplainingly, like job hunters. There is often a certain careless joy to substituting, something you might not expect; usually there's a stool to sit on, and the day is planned for you: hand this out, read these pages. There are no great responsibilities, and the classroom door is open to the hall, so from other parts of the school come the sounds of real labor — teachers and students talking, buses pulling up and leaving, the big doors slamming shut in the gymnasium.

That afternoon I heard Turner across the hall, talking to his class. There came a long pause, a flash of light, a sharp cracking sound — then a yelp of pleasure, an excited babble. Next, Turner's voice, dry and serious: "Don't go trying this at home." My own students looked up sluggishly from their desks, like cattle noticing the rain.

The director was Don Hamand. Don, thirty, was a bearded John Lennon type who made his own ice cream and brought it to rehearsal in stainless steel buckets. He was married, and occasionally his wife came by, wearing their baby on her back. She made suggestions now and then in a high, child's voice, the voice of a cartoon. Don sat far away, in the back row, in the dark, and shouted out directions. From the stage he was invisible. "Hey! I can't *hear* you!" he'd say. "You're supposed to step *forward*, goddammit! *Forward!*" You'd look around and there'd be nobody.

When I wasn't climbing around in the rafters I spent a lot of time sitting in the back with Don, holding his clipboard and taking notes for him. "My wife and I are having another baby," he said one night, watching the stage.

"Congratulations."

"Yeah, I don't know. I'm not making any money." He sighed. "I need another job."

"You've got that DJ job still."

"Yeah. I hate it. Keeps me up all night."

I said, "Turner wants me to write in a nude scene."

"Jesus Christ."

"You know anything about her husband?"

"Janine?" Don winced and shifted in his seat. "Yeah, Ray Lunk.

They should have sent him up the river, that guy. She's embarrassed about it, I think."

"Yeah."

"She's a pill, you know. But terrific. Beautiful."

"Janine is."

"*Hell*, yes," Don said. "Look at her."

She stood in blue light on stage. Her black ringlets fell over her face.

He said, "I mean, I love my wife. I don't want to say anything. But you can't deny it."

"Sure."

"Another baby." He sighed again. "You can't imagine what this is like for me."

During this time I was living in a house on the coast, in a little town called Florence, about an hour's drive from Eugene. The house belonged to my aunt Petta, who had moved to Jamaica, and I paid no rent. *I'm having a tropical crisis!* Petta said, and off she went. I didn't know her well, but I remembered her from childhood as a well-dressed woman who wore wide-brimmed hats and sat in an iron chair on our lawn. She was rich through marriage, had worked for an auction house, and had seen marvelous things pass through her office. Well, she would say. Let's just say I could tell you some *things* about the Rijksmuseum. Don't *tell* me you don't know about the new Caillebotte, she once said, a hand on my arm.

She asked me to look after her house — I was living in Eugene, teaching, when she left the country — and I moved in my few things. It was a huge cedar-shake house on a cliff above the ocean. Moss grew on the roof, and fir trees dripped and scraped against the windows. I didn't use much of the house, and it was a little unnerving, all that emptiness at my back, unseen rooms full of dark coastal furniture, the old Nooksak blankets heavy on the walls, a big stone fireplace. A wooden stairway went down to the beach, which was rocky and unforgiving, and always windy, but away in a little grotto I found Petta's ratty old towels, a rusty aluminum chair, an empty wine bottle.

Janine Richardson called me at home a week before opening night. She said, "You're not busy?"

"Not me," I said.

"Well, I'm in a strange mood," she said, flatly. "I'm all *antsy.* I get this way before an opening. You ever get superstitious?"

"No."

"Oh, hell, I am. That makes us incompatible."

"No, come on out," I said. It was late and foggy, and I didn't expect anything. "If you want. It's nice out here tonight."

"All right," she said, "give me some directions," and an hour later she pulled her Citroën up the driveway. It was ten o'clock, and the junipers in the yard were filled with mist. She looked nervously one way, then the other, before coming up the stairs. "You look tired," she said, stomping past me. She was wearing a brown dress that went only to her knees.

"Been working."

"Sure you have." She put her satchel down, changed her mind and picked it up, slung it over her shoulder. "I might need this." She clasped it to her. She wore a dusty, noncommittal perfume, and her hair was piled on top of her head.

She followed me into the living room, where a long polished table sat like a reflecting pool. On the walls were photographs of Petta's father in his goggles, driving. Janine cruised past the pictures, then walked to the windows and peered out at the dark yard.

"This isn't your house," she said.

"It's my aunt's."

"Where's your aunt?" She turned to me.

"Jamaica," I said. I explained the rest.

"Nice arrangement."

I followed her into the dining room. From behind she seemed foreign and unapproachable. Her neck was long, and little wisps of her hair clung to it. I showed her the dining room table, where I kept my typewriter and papers — papers stacked in piles, some math tests I'd just finished grading, empty beer bottles, my books about Edison.

"Ah ha," she said. "You used all these books?" She rummaged through the biographies, letting her satchel swing free. There was a section of photographs, and she pored over it for a while and said, "These are his kids?"

"Your kids," I said.

"Ha ha."

I looked over her shoulder. Mary Stilwell was standing there in a flowery bonnet. Janine touched her hair.

"Well, would you look at me," she said.

Her daughter, Dot, was lithe and cottony and stood in the garden with her hands shading her eyes, looking as if she could slide effortlessly out of the frame, like a swan; her sons, William and Thomas, were staid and fearful, and looked at the camera respectfully, their arms hanging stiff at their sides. But Mary, their mother, was the dark grave beauty of the picture. With a little age she was becoming larger, assuming a matronly width and complacence.

"You were very pretty."

"Oh, in my day." She laughed, a lovely sound, lovely in the way she was on stage, generous and unquestioning.

"Something to drink?"

"Beer. I just got out of class."

"Teacher," I said.

"Yeah, well." She lit a cigarette. "You don't mind?"

I gave her a bottle of Henry's.

"You didn't put the kids in the play."

"Child actors," I said.

"Fuff." She drank her beer and smoked her cigarette. "You know I was married before."

"Turner told me."

"What'd he say?"

I told her the story he'd told me. She smoked and stared at the dark window, watching herself reflected there. When I was done, she said, "Well, yeah, that's pretty accurate." She tipped her ashes onto my math tests. "Except it was a Lincoln. The Lunk," she said, grimly. "I married him in high school."

"High school?"

"He was handsome. How was I supposed to know he'd be a criminal?"

"How long did he get?"

She glared at me. "It's really none of your business."

"I guess not," I said. "Turner thinks you don't like him."

"Oh, no, he's okay." She finished her cigarette. "But he's lonely, and it worries me. I see myself ending up that way, you know? Old and sloppy." She looked down at herself and brushed ashes from her lap with the side of her hand. She considered her dress. "This is the best I can do these days, you know. This little thing."

"It's nice."

"I used to do better."

"Let me show you the house," I said.

"Deal." She stood up.

I took her upstairs. I could feel her behind me, watching as I walked ahead of her. In the big hallway we stopped, and she looked from side to side, like someone coming up from a subway entrance. "Lordy," she said, "this place goes on, doesn't it?"

"Six bedrooms up here."

"You rotate?" she said. She flicked her eyebrows up, saucily. "One a day? Rest on Sundays?"

"I haven't had sex in so long," I said.

"Oh, my God. Don't tell me these things." She looked alarmed. The door to the attic was ajar. She opened it and peered up the rickety stairs, holding her satchel against her hip. "What's up there?"

"The attic."

"Where's your bedroom?"

"Down there." I pointed.

"When's your aunt coming back?"

"Probably not today."

We walked down the hall into the bedroom. From the windows during the day I could see the beach; the lighthouse on the headland to the north winked around and around. There was a good wind blowing, and the glass in the windows shivered and bowed.

She plopped down on my bed. "Nice quilt."

"Thanks." I walked to the windows, nervously. Her dress had hiked itself up her thighs. Her legs were smooth and pale. I pointed at the ceiling. "At night I hear people walking back and forth up there," I said. "Doors close by themselves. Sometimes I hear two women talking, but there's no one around. It gets a little creepy."

"You're so full of shit."

"Seriously," I said.

She stood up and walked to the window, her flat shoes scuffing the floor. Her dress settled back to her knees. She was standing next to me. "I was wondering if you'd write me a different ending," she said.

"This is about that?"

"For some reason I don't like the idea of dying. That's what I mean when I say I'm superstitious. I don't like dying on stage."

"But she died."

"I know she died," she said. "This is totally unprofessional of me."

"There's only a week left."

"I know. Just a tiny scene. Five minutes. It's bad luck to die on stage. I've already talked to Don about it, it's okay with him. He said you might make me a ghost."

"All right."

"Or something. Or write me out entirely, I don't know. Just at the end, I mean, not the whole thing." She gritted her teeth and tried to smile. "Please?"

"Okay."

"Promise?"

"Sure. I promise."

"Because if you don't," she said, "I'm thinking of quitting." She kissed my cheek, a brief peck, and turned to go.

"That's it?"

"For now," she said, looking away.

"Criminy," I said.

"Take nothing for granted, dear heart," she said. "It's the worst thing you can do."

I didn't have much to say to that. I led her down the stairs and outside, and from the porch I watched her car make the road, the headlights bob away.

Monday after school Turner and I went around stapling posters to telephone poles, passing out flyers in the grocery stores. The posters showed Edison leaning over a worktable, a halo of light above him. Mary stood off to the side, looking away, off the page. Hello, darling, Turner said, bowing to the shoppers. He was in costume, and tapped his shiny shoe on the grocery store linoleum. He'd frosted his hair, and stray white dots speckled his forehead. People took the flyers anyway. Then after rehearsal we went down to the tavern.

Now we were on our fifth round, and Turner hadn't changed clothes.

"Mr. Edison," I said.

"Yessir," he said.

"The governor of mysterious invisible forces."

"Hell, yes." He picked at his lip.

"You're not married, are you."

"Me? Nah. Not in real life."

"Never been?"

"No. Well, yeah, once. Long, long time ago." He puffed out his cheeks. "Big mistake."

"Why's that."

"Too young." He was squinting at his beer. "There's this woman I'm seeing now, though," he said. "Nobody knows but you. And her, of course. And me. We're keeping it a secret." He spun the bottle on its base. "You know *why* it's a secret?"

"Why."

He stared at me, drunk. "Because she's sixty years old." He held the stare. "She's a young sixty, but she's way the fuck older than me."

"Where'd you meet her?"

"I met her on vacation when I was in Costa Rica." He leaned toward me and whispered, "She's from Portland. Also, she's still married. But she's getting divorced. Her husband doesn't know."

"No shit?"

"No shit." Turner nodded gravely.

"The husband's an asshole," I said.

"Maybe, maybe not," Turner said. "She gives me her side of the story, I know there's another side, this poor guy working all day, his wife going off on vacation by herself. No, I do feel kind of bad." He cleared his throat. "But I've got to take what I can get, at this point."

He was still wearing his striped vest and watch chain and the dirty white spats over his shoes. His hair stood up in front. I had stolen Janine's black nylon choker and wore it doubled around my wrist like a rubber band.

"The hell is that."

"Janine's," I said. "I stole it."

He reached for my wrist. "Let me smell it I'll buy another round."

"I've got to get up in the morning."

"Please." He reached for it again.

"I'm teaching gym somewhere."

"One more," he said. He grabbed me and smelled my wrist, his big hand holding mine.

We had long dress rehearsals that last week, staying until well after midnight. We practiced the new ending until we were all in a terrible mood; we began to pick on one another. Don had hemorrhoids and had to sit on a padded cushion ring, and, off stage, Janine treated Turner the way I remembered treating outcasts in high school, turning blithely away when he spoke, rolling her eyes. He looked even more haggard than usual: V-neck sweaters with no undershirt, his neck thick and sweaty.

When things got especially bad, I'd make for the rafters. Below me, on stage, Mary touched Edison's arm and leaned deferentially toward him in a perfect simulation of adoration. She followed him across the stage, time after time, finding the right blue light to stop in; she spoke calmly to reporters, nodding, biting her lips with pride. Then she'd go heavily off the stage and put on her overcoat and smoke in the front row. Her ashes marked the red carpet like erasures.

"Looking good," I called down to her.

She smirked up at me, still wearing her bonnet and high black boots. "Forget it," she said.

By Tuesday night the weather had turned crappy again, raining and blowing, the streetlights swinging over the intersections downtown. I met Janine outside the theater, and we went in together. I turned on a few lights, plugged in the coffee pot, and we sat in the front row, waiting. From somewhere we heard a heavy rumbling that could have been thunder, or a train, or maybe just the old building grumbling at us, settling on its haunches.

She said, "I like the new ending. It's a very powerful feeling." She put her hand on my arm. "Let me see if I can describe it to you."

A door slammed in the basement.

"Someone's here," I said.

"It's very *lib*erating." She licked her lips, thoughtfully, gazing over my shoulder. "Not in the usual sense."

Someone came walking upstairs, banging heavy shoes.

She leaned closer. "It's a little ex*cit*ing, if you know what I mean."

She shrugged slowly, rolling her shoulders inside her coat. "I like coming up behind him like that. That's what it is. It's secret power. That's what I like about it. Nobody knows who you are."

A door opened in the back of the auditorium.

"I want to see you tonight," she said.

I shivered. "All right."

"I'm coming out to your place." Her hand was on my forearm now, steady. She gave me a squeeze. "After rehearsal tonight?"

"Sure," I said.

"I'll bring you a little surprise."

Turner clomped down the aisle, singing, already in costume. We watched him pour a cup of coffee, his wide butt toward us. "Evening," he said, happily.

"Evening."

He motioned to me, waved me over.

"What?"

"Come here," Turner said, and I walked toward him. The coffee machine hissed and popped. He leaned over and whispered in my ear, a big meaty hand on my cheek. "She did it," he said. "She's divorcing the guy." He was grinning like a fool, and he lifted his cup and toasted himself. "How's that?" he said. "Here's to me."

One of Edison's rivals, an insane inventor named Nikola Tesla, once said that had it not been for Mary Stilwell's constant attention, Edison would have died of neglect — that he didn't eat, didn't wash, couldn't keep himself in new clothes. But every Fourth of July Edison woke his family by throwing firecrackers into a barrel on the lawn, and in rainy weather he put coins on the tops of metal poles and had his boys shinny up. He blew water on his children's faces from a tiny glass swan. We imagine him insistent and artless in love, but what about the notes to himself in his notebooks? *My wife Popsy-Wopsy can't invent,* he wrote. He bought her long trailing satin dresses, which she quickly outgrew as she fattened. True, he read the *Police Gazette* at the dinner table, and he was disappointed in his sons, who were weaklings, and he often slept in the laboratory. But after Mary died, before she was thirty, he avoided Menlo Park, and when, years later, he married again, he married only for station and elegance, his knuckles clean, his hair well tended. Who's to say he loved badly or ungratefully? How can we forget the first time our souls are lit with this mysterious flame?

Janine followed me home that night, her headlights caught in my rearview mirror all the way out to the coast. We parked in the driveway and went down the wooden staircase to the beach. A terrific wind was blowing, plastering my shirt to my chest, and Janine held her coat closed and shielded her eyes. We walked along the beach, on the rocks, picking our way through the driftwood, until we came to Petta's little grotto, where we could talk without shouting. Janine sat in one of the lawn chairs and I sat in the other. The black ceiling arched over us, wet and dripping. A black pool of seawater sat nearby, and from far away we could hear the waves banging in and out of some other hole in the rock, hollow-barrel sounds.

"This is a good place," she said. "Come here often?"

"No," I said. "Only once."

"Good except for this being empty." She rolled the wine bottle toward me.

We sat quietly, listening to the wind. I told Janine what happened after she died: she was buried beneath a tree in Menlo Park, I said, and her picture ran front page in the papers. The laboratory shut down, and black bunting hung from the windows. "Oh, that's sad," she said, absently. She patted my arm as if it were the most natural thing. She watched the surf crawl out of the ocean. On the horizon we saw the orange lights of a freighter.

"I hope you understand why I didn't want to do that," she said. "I know it's stupid, but it seems like it'd just be asking for trouble."

"Doesn't matter to me."

"It's superstitious and juvenile." She kicked the bottle into the water, then leaned forward and plucked it out again. "It is."

"I guess it is," I said. "I think it's turned out fine."

"You're sweet to say so." She sighed. "You know that Lunk guy did me in for a long time. We both used to drive around in that thing, you know? Just sitting there, riding along in this car, and it was supposed to be somebody's lunches or something. I still feel like a shitheel for that."

"He remarried?"

"Oh yes." She stretched her legs in front of her and regarded them in the dark. "Twice."

"Edison remarried," I said. "Had some more kids. Two, I think."

"Asshole."

"No, no, no. He was lonely," I said, though of course that wasn't quite it.

The wind was cool and fishy. The waves bonked around in the back of the grotto.

"I brought that bonnet with me," she said.

"You did not."

"I did. That's the surprise." She faced me now, almost entirely invisible in the dark. "I knew you liked it, you sleazeball," she said. "I saw you staring at me."

"I was enthralled with your acting."

"Ha," she said, and turned away. "I brought one of those dresses, too."

"Oh, my."

"You like those," she said.

"You know me too well."

"And I brought you a little vest I found. I thought you might be interested."

I leaned over the aluminum arm of my chair and tried to kiss her, but she tilted away. "Huh. Fat chance," she said. She took my hand and walked us back up the beach, the sand wet and firm under our feet.

"I don't have any spats," I said.

"Always be prepared," she said. She ran up the wooden stairs, two steps at a time, her hair wild in the wind. I walked slowly after her. "Wimp," she said, at the top. She was gasping.

The house stood empty above us, two rooms lit up. The light spilled onto the gravel driveway.

"That's a big place," she said. She put her hands on her hips and stared up at it, as she might stare at an office building. Then she went to her Citroën, which sat like a bug in the driveway, and opened the trunk. She took out a blue dress with a black bow and a pair of floppy lace-up boots. The boots were black, and the laces dangled over the car's bumper. "You like?" she asked.

"Very nice."

She draped the dress over her arm. "Here's your vest." She handed me a striped, satiny vest with small black buttons.

I slipped into it and fastened the buttons. It hung on me like a shawl.

"Oh," she said, "you look terrible." She peered at me, then into the trunk of the car. "That's all I have."

I shoved out my stomach. "How about this?"

Suddenly she laughed, that beautiful, clear sound. "Cut it out."

I led her to the porch and inside. The light in the front hall was bright and frank.

"Just a minute," she said. She took the clothes and disappeared into the bathroom.

In the kitchen I found a Styrofoam cup, split it in half, and fitted one half over each of my shoes. They squeaked. I marched from one end of the house to the other, up and down in front of the windows.

"Spats," I said, when she came out.

"Good." She had her hair bundled on top of her head. She was lovely. She had somehow darkened her eyes, and her dress fit her wonderfully, tight at her waist. She spun to show me the back. "Lace me up."

"I don't think that's the idea."

She shook her shoulders at me. "Do it."

I laced her up. "This is a shoelace."

"I couldn't find anything else. It's two shoelaces tied together."

I tied the strings in a bow. She drew in her stomach and turned around. Strands of her dark hair waved in the air like antennae. She smiled and tipped her head back, showing her throat. In her antique dress she was smooth and mannerly.

I took the choker from my pocket. "Put this on," I said.

"Ah ha. You psycho." She snapped it into place. "Like my boots?" she asked, holding out one foot. She grasped my shoulder for balance, and I put my hand on her hand: it was cool and bony and studded with rings.

"Very nice."

She walked to the window. "Show me your books again," she said.

"All right." I led her through the bright rooms to the dining room.

"Sit down," she said. "Pretend you don't see me. Pretend to work."

I looked at her reflection in the windows. She was standing behind me, hands on her hips, the way I regarded my students, I suppose, waiting for misbehavior, not really minding if it occurred.

"You can't look at me," she said. "Study. Pretend you're working. It's important."

"All right." I opened my books, one after the other, and she left the room. I heard her walk away, into the kitchen. I tapped a pencil. I heard her slam a door, walk farther away, into the living room, the kitchen, then far away, into the hallway, until I couldn't hear her anymore.

I stayed sitting. I looked at the pictures. Here was Edison, grumpy and sleepless at his phonograph, his cuffs black and torn; here he was on the lawn, in the sun, reading a book in a chair; here he was in the machine shop, hunched over and glowering at his workers; here he was climbing a ladder to retrieve a jar; here he was sitting at his desk, reading a book. His big, weathered head, set like a stone in its starchy collar; his wide, ungainly rear; his white hat sitting on his desk like a plate while he shows a movie, leaning forward into the projector, his eye aligned with something out of the frame. She breathed on my neck.

"Is this what you like?" she asked.

Here she stood under a tree, holding a parasol; here, in bright sunlight, she sat in the stern of a rowboat, holding the sides firmly; here she gazed curiously into a book, holding her two sons on her lap. Here she stood and looked placidly out at me. She raised her chin.

"Do you like this?" She put her nose on my collar. "Where is your soul?" she asked. "Is it here?" She breathed into my ear. I kept my eyes down. She touched my cheek, the corner of my lips. She ran her finger over my chin. "Is it here?" A dark red curtain rising in my mind. She lifted her arms to me, an apparition. "Is it here?"

# In the Kingdom of Prester John

IN THE SPRING when I was seventeen, my cousin Ron the map-maker went off his medicine and disappeared from work at the ferry terminal. My mother and I took the electric trolley down to his waterfront office and found his drafting desk clean under the fluorescent lights, his mechanical pencils and X-acto knives snapped neatly into their black plastic cases. On his tilted draftsman's desk was a half-drawn map of the Tacoma Narrows, a long sleeve of water reaching for the bottom of the paper. He had penciled in fathom figures, but only delicately. His coffee cup on the filing cabinet was half full and very cold. Where had he gone? No one knew. His co-workers frowned their bearded faces and shrugged. Unlike my cousin, they looked harsh, like men of the sea.

"Oh, for chrissake," my mother said. She smoked in those days. "Just when you think you've got your bases covered."

"Sorry," they said. But he had disappeared before.

My mother and I took the trolley to his house on Capitol Hill. He had inherited the house — an old brick Victorian — from his mother. The shades were drawn and the lawn was green and fragrant and the rhododendrons were blooming, big and fleshy. From the sidewalk everything appeared to be in order.

An old woman on the neighboring porch called to us. "Say," she said, waving, "I've got Ron's mail." She disappeared, then reappeared with a paper grocery sack, which she brought to us. "Is he on a trip?"

"We don't know. We're looking for him."

"I'm not a snoop," the old woman said. Her eyes were hard and yellow, and she was skinny. "So I certainly wouldn't know where he is."

"The man is my relation," said my mother. "He's missing."

"He's a little strange, you know."

"Yes," my mother said, and tucked the sack of mail under her arm. "We know he's strange."

"Frankly, I don't think he should be allowed out."

"Well, go ahead and write your congressman," my mother said, and blew smoke at her.

My mother had a key, so we went in. Dark yellow light seeped through the parchment shades. The rooms were gold and glowing. The oak floors shone. I expected my cousin to be dead somewhere, his head cracked open on the sink, maybe. He'd always been clumsy — or afflicted, really: electroshock, insulin shock, a hundred different drugs. But instead, we found all his furniture turned upside down. The dark, carved legs of the dining room table curled into the air like well-muscled arms. The long brown buffet was on its back, its white china plates and saucers stacked neatly on the rug. All the chairs in the house were upside down, too: the black vinyl bar stools, the green leather chairs by the fireplace, the piano bench — it was as if everything had floated to the ceiling and crashed down again. We walked slowly through the house, amazed, though Ron tended to do such things now and then.

In the bathroom we found the sink plugged with a washcloth and the washcloth weighted with a big orange brick that had scratched the enamel. A plywood board covered the mouth of the toilet bowl. The showerhead was wrapped in a blue plastic shopping bag, which was secured with a rubber band.

"Jeez," I said.

My mother fluffed her hair in the mirror. She was just starting to age, and she pushed curiously at the bags under her eyes. She said, "I'd say this is definitely a new pinnacle of weirdness." Casually she removed the plastic bag from around the showerhead, folded it, and put it in her purse; she took the rubber band, too, snapping it around her wrist. She considered the brick, but left it.

"This is a nice house," I said, back downstairs. It was many years since I'd been there. Ron was far, far richer than we were. Dark beams supported the living room ceiling. A painting of Ron's grandfather hung above the fireplace. The glass in the leaded windows, when I looked closely, was pinched and swimmy. "Look at this," I said.

"Well, I guess you didn't know that glass is actually a liquid." My mother ran her fingers over the panes. "It just flows very slowly. These windows are so old they're probably a little thicker on the bottom."

"Huh," I said.

"Now you know," she said.

"Guess I do."

"But don't go wanting what you can't have," she said.

"I don't," I said.

"You'd better not," she said. She was a librarian, and she'd saved her money for years so she could pay for my first year of college the next fall, but after that, it was understood, I would fend for myself. It was a fair deal, looking back. My father wasn't around — off in Chicago, last we'd heard, newly married — but my uncles were fishermen in Alaska, and most years they made good money, some of which my mother accepted quietly, though she hated to do it. My uncles had made offers. I was strong and tall; I could work six weeks fishing in the summer, three more crabbing in the winter, and make eight thousand dollars, a lot of money in those days. And the wilderness appealed to me, in a sort of all-American way — eagles, bears, the fat silver fish. I imagined the scenes you saw printed on sleeping bags, if you had sleeping bags, which I didn't. And I wanted to travel, too — adolescent feelings, really, I put no stock in them now, these longings for travel and adventure. A friend of mine would be going to Mexico for the summer, and that sounded interesting: lots of sun, the women with their round breasts sleeping naked in the afternoon. I'd got these ideas from books, and I knew they couldn't be entirely true, but they intrigued me. They were away from home, and I had the idea that I shouldn't be hanging around much longer. I suppose I was anxious about almost everything in those days.

In Ron's darkened study we found his drafting table upright, maybe the only upright thing in the house. The desk was maplewood, identical to his table at work, a black desk lamp screwed to the side. Six or seven sheets of beautiful white paper lay, untouched, on the desk. I flipped through them, and they rattled, a bare, windy sound in the quiet house. "Oh, good Lord," my mother said, exasperated. She stared angrily at a jar of pencils. She looked as though she wanted to kick the table over, for consistency's sake.

In the sack of mail were three newspapers still wrapped in their rubber bands, a phone bill, and five brochures from exterminators. "Goddamn that nuthead," my mother said, fanning through them. "He's worried about *bugs* now." She dropped his mail on the hall table and started to leave. "Wait a minute," she said, and disappeared. She came back with a silver serving spoon, long and ornate, which she slipped into her purse. "I deserve *something* out of this."

On the wide porch she patted my shoulder. Did she think this was difficult for me? It was unnerving, yes, but fascinating, too, like gossip. And it had happened before. He would turn up eventually; he always did. Outside, his new blue Ford sat in the driveway, empty and spotless. We went home and called the police.

In bed that night I wondered: Where would he go? He'd never been afraid of bugs before, though I guess he'd always been afraid of the possibilities the world presented. And why had he stopped taking his medicine? He'd never been so thorough before, so absolutely destructive. He'd only insisted my name was Walter, when it's not; he'd watched things hovering over the table when there was nothing to see. He had always been strange, his eyes too wide, too eager, and his hair never quite right. His memory had been shot to hell by the electroshock. But he'd usually known what was real and what wasn't; he'd given me scarves and checks at Christmas, and he had season tickets for the Huskies, which made him aristocracy in our eyes, and aristocracy was allowed its eccentricities. Now I had to wonder what he imagined was crawling around his house. Orange-and-black beetles? Tiny yellow-bodied flies? I could picture him tiptoeing down the halls, playing Shark with the rugs and the floors. Could I imagine believing what he did — that my house was filling with bugs, like a bucket filling with sand? We all have momentary visions of madness, when the world is too profuse or too chaotic to be named, I knew that even then. Outside, the trees shivered like paper. Somewhere in the neighborhood a car started. Through the open window I smelled the Oroweat bakery across the lake. It was May, and warm.

The house creaked and popped like a ship, and I thought of it rocking slowly one way, then the other, on high-walled seas, or I tried to imagine this happening; but my body was stiff and flat as a board, and the house was still. Maybe when Ron lay in bed he became the house, and maybe he felt the insects crawling along his arms and up the back of his neck. Could you imagine being a house when you weren't a house? Could you imagine being a ship if you weren't at sea? I tried to see masts sprouting from my chest, growing like trees, setting out sails, my sails ballooning in a sudden breeze from the window, a keel growing down from my back and burrowing into the bed. For a moment, a frightening moment, I could feel myself spinning slowly in a tide, a soft lazy motion; but then a dog ran by, barking, chasing something into the bushes. "Doris," said a man's voice, and off they went down the sidewalk.

The next day I had my final in history. Like all our finals, it was in the auditorium, where the seats were purple velour, where we used tiny folding tables that attached to the armrests. We each had two pencils, which we had sharpened to needles, and we had dressed for the occasion, some of us: white shirts, a few ties; you remember. We made a low-level roar sitting there, waiting.

I spotted Carl, a friend, staring at the cover of his calculus final, his crew-cut head bent down. I called his name, and he turned. "What say, Tom?" he said.

"You ready?"

He said, "Hell's bells."

"Good luck."

"Fast fighting," he said.

The assistant principal was in charge, a fat Italian man, Mr. Fratiorno, a man we all called Burger. He stood on stage, in front of a huge purple curtain, which breathed slowly in and out like a benign underwater animal. "You may begin," he said, holding his tie.

So I flipped through the exam. There were three questions, and we were to choose one; I'd studied African colonization, and there it was: *Discuss some of the myths that drove Europeans to explore Africa.* My palms started sweating, and I wiped them on my pants.

At one point when somebody nudged me I realized I'd been humming, lost in my work. In my imagination the European Christians —

in their buckled armor and swooping helmets, and polishing their new long guns — sailed close along the coast of Western Africa, peering through the trees for the hint of a river of diamonds or an ocean of sand, things they'd all heard about. The long equatorial days passed, hot and still. From their ships at night, anchored in a stifling unpopulated harbor, they heard peeps and murmurs from the shore, a low, bright river of sound. *There run in our country blue horses,* Prester John had written. *And white bears, and peculiar lions of red, green, black, and blue color. And be it known to you that in our skies are birds called gryphons, who can carry an ox or a man into their high nests to feed their young. And be it known to you also that in part of our country are peculiar men who have human bodies but the heads of dogs, whose language can never be learned, yet they are good fishermen, as they can swim the deepest seas a day without emerging.* On deck the sailors slept on their backs, facing the clouds. In the cool mornings the sailors looked for seagulls, whose wheeling paths would mark the mouths of rivers. I wrote and wrote.

That afternoon I met Carl in the park for basketball. He was very good — sturdy and quick and four inches taller than I was. The court was hard-packed dirt, and two roots humped under the basket, so occasionally the ball went rolling onto the grass or under the trees. The day was overcast but warm, weather that made my joints ache. Traffic swished by.

"Did you go preregister last week?" he asked, leaning over, hands on his knees. His glasses slid down his nose.

"No. Did you?"

"Got all my classes picked out," he said.

"What are you taking?"

"Calculus, economics, couple government classes." He sank a left-handed shot from the foul line. "Left-a-lee," he said. "Went up and checked out my dorm room, too."

"You've got a room?"

"Yeah," he said. "It's low budget. No view."

"How'd you get a room?"

"You go show your papers and you get a room. You should try to get into a co-ed dorm, man. It's amazing. College does something to girls."

The ball rolled away under a tree. I picked it up and walked back to the court.

"They are so good-looking," he said.

"High budget?" I asked.

"Very high budget."

"No kidding."

"They're open today, if you want to go over and look around. I'll give you a ride."

"No thanks," I said. But what was I scared of? I suppose I was scared of leaving home. I could imagine the dormitory carpets, stained and feral smelling; the windows sealed shut; a foreign squalor. "I'll go later," I said.

Back home, my mother was cutting tomatoes. "Did you know that in some cultures, a woman will name her baby while she's falling asleep, to make sure she gets the right name?" Her hands were shiny with oil. "Isn't that perfect?"

I rolled the basketball into the closet.

"Also, I learned something else today. Sometimes, when a ship sinks, its buoyancy is just right, and it doesn't sink all the way, it just floats halfway down." She stirred lettuce with her fingers. "Two things today."

I cleared my throat and washed my hands. Brown water ran down the drain. What was I feeling? I felt off balance, as if I'd forgotten something.

"They'll find him," she said. "They always find him."

"I know," I said.

"He'll be fine," she said. "Or, not fine. But you know. Back to before."

"I know," I said again. I was a little concerned; she was right about that. And madness ran in our family, after all. I was just about that age. Two grandparents, an uncle, a cousin, all crazy in one way or another. So I wasn't out of the woods yet, you could say, and I worried a lot about my own well-being. But I found it hard to worry about Ron. He was a smart man — everyone said so — full of vigor, and I liked to think of him out there now, out in the city, making his way.

*　　*　　*

Three days later my cousin Ron turned up in the middle of Empire Avenue, walking, his hands outstretched like a blind man's. The police picked him up and brought him to Western State, and there he got back on his medicine, and a week later he went home. My mother and I helped him rearrange his furniture. He was in his thirties but looked far older: balding, gray hair, baggy gray institutional shirt. Even in his own house he looked dazed and unshaven, as if he'd just stepped off a plane. He stood back and watched us pick everything up, turn it over, and set it down. When I went around pulling up the shades, he winced at the light. My mother started knocking around in the kitchen, fixing him dinner. Where had he been all that time? I dusted my hands off. He sat gingerly on the sofa, folding and refolding his hands.

After a minute he said, "Tom?"

"Yeah?" I said.

"That sunlight," he said, "makes the room seem bigger."

"I know it does," I said.

"Everything opens," he said.

I looked around the room. Particles of dust hung in the air.

"You're right," I said. "It does."

"But I don't mind." He clasped his hands together with finality and squinted up at me. "No, I'm happy to say I don't mind it, not at all."

# Dirigibles

HOWARD AND LOUISE walked arm in arm down the tilted field, and when they were forty feet from the beehives they stopped, because at this point Louise was usually tired, and because Howard knew this was as close as Louise liked to get. She leaned heavily on his arm, breathing. It was August, so it was warm in the dry field, and a flat mountain heat rose from the grass.

She said, "Just a minute."

"Yep," Howard said.

She arched her back and cleared her throat and sighed. She was a short round woman with gray hair and a prominent nose, and she'd been sick for some time with multiple sclerosis; these days she found it difficult to walk. Her clavicle stood out under her clothes like a handle, and her feet were long and narrow in their sneakers. For a long moment they stood together in the field. Around them, in the deep, late-afternoon light, Howard could see his bees — they hovered here and there over the pasture, like a handful of pebbles that had been tossed into the air and hadn't come down.

"I'll just wait," she said, "over here." She leaned against the fence.

Howard picked up his things and went off toward the beehives. He worried about his wife; even on her good days she was tiring more easily. It was hard to see unless you'd been with her a long time, but he could see it.

At the beehives Howard pulled on his gloves and lowered his helmet onto his head. Then he knelt, and carefully, as though sliding fragile mail out of a box, pulled out a long shelf of bees. They crawled earnestly over his gloves, up and down his stubby fingers, hundreds of them, little balls of yellow thread that ambled around the frame of the shelf and flew off aimlessly, looping around his head, landing on his plastic helmet. He loved them for the dependable way they flew out and back every day; they were admirable, he thought. He liked the sweet, electric smell of the bees, too, an odor that rose now from the dark interior of the hive. He pushed them delicately off his gloves and collected a jarful of honey, and when he slid the shelf back in, a few bees went shooting away over the field. He walked back to his wife, carrying the jar, warm in his hand.

"They gave me a deal," he said, holding it up. "Half off."

"You've got a bee in there."

"Ah-ha," he said. He reached in and scooped it out, dead, with his finger, and wiped it on the grass. "So they sold me a bill of goods."

They walked back toward the house, their long shadows stretched in front of them. His old rounded tractor lay under a tarp in a corner of the field, and their house, an A-frame he had built himself, stood at the top of the field, high and triangular against the dark woods. He'd been well organized in his life, Howard had, but recently he'd begun to let things go. He hadn't looked at the tractor in months and had almost forgotten it was there. He had been forgetting lots of things lately, and it frightened him, as though everything was, decisively, beginning to come apart. He and Louise didn't answer the phone sometimes, and that bothered him, too; after it stopped ringing and the house was quiet again, he felt as though a big hole had been torn in the day. Not that it was ever anyone important. Their kids never called. But it was unsettling, as though they had decided to step aside from things.

Louise let go of his arm and walked along beside him, lifting one narrow foot out of the grass, then the other. After a minute of this she took up his arm again.

"I'm not looking forward to tonight," she said.

"He's a nice guy. You remember him."

"No, I don't," she said. "I don't remember him at all."

"We'll stay out of your way, if you want."

"Well." She lifted the hem of her dress and examined her sneakers. "By all means, don't mind me."

James Couch, a friend of theirs from the old days, was coming to dinner, driving over from Seattle and leaving again the next morning — he would stay in a motel — on his way to Montana to see his daughter. Howard and James Couch had worked together on the ferries, in Seattle, years ago. Howard had been a ferry captain, and James Couch had worked alongside him, his first mate, for three years, before Couch got his own boat. They hadn't been all that close — Howard hadn't liked making friends at work — but Howard and Louise didn't have many friends anymore, so Howard didn't feel he could be choosy.

He set up his film projector in the living room and stacked his film cans, like thick, impossible coins, beside it. After assuring himself it was entirely clean, he tacked a white sheet to the living room wall. He had movies of the ferry days, which he supposed James Couch would like; Howard himself hadn't seen them in years. He'd more or less forgotten what was on them.

"Oh, Howard, not those," Louise said, peering in, examining the labels.

"Why not?"

"Show him some slides or something."

"He's my friend," Howard said, "and I'll show him what I want."

"You don't even remember what's on those."

"Of course I do."

"Well," Louise said, and shrugged. "Okey-dokey." She hobbled out of the room.

So Howard waited. He sat on the porch in a lawn chair. He opened a bottle of beer and drank it slowly, watching the sun set behind the trees. A hummingbird approached the porch and darted away. They'd been lucky to get the place when they had, twenty years ago, when no one wanted to live on the hot, unsophisticated side of the mountains; they'd ended up with a lot of land they couldn't possibly have afforded if they were buying today. Now there were espresso stands in town, even here, run by girls in green aprons — he wouldn't have thought it, but Howard actually liked driving down to town in the mornings and getting two coffees and bringing them back with the paper. It was a small life and, he thought, a good one. They'd planted a row of apple trees and grew their own vegetables, and now that he had retired from the ferries they lived here from March to October, returning to their little house in Seattle just as the rainy season started and avoiding the snow that fell heavily here in Roslyn. Howard liked the snow, but it was hard to get around in, especially with Louise.

Howard didn't mind his wife's illness, not exactly, though he would never have said as much out loud — he mostly enjoyed taking what care of her he could. It wasn't much. She had her good days and bad. He vacuumed now, which he'd never done before. He did the laundry. He'd traded in their stick shift for an automatic, because Louise could no longer use the clutch, and every morning in the city he got on his bony ten-speed bicycle and rode around the lake for exercise, admiring his tall, long-legged shadow, like a spider under his black helmet. His knees ached and yellow spots flashed in his eyes when he climbed the hills, but on he went. He loved his wife, and the fact made him feel good; but she unnerved him a little, too. My leg, she might say; I can't move my leg. And they'd both look at it there, under her hands.

A car appeared at the bottom of the pasture and made its way slowly up the road, bucking and tossing. It was an old rusty car the color of grass, with a luggage rack on top. Howard went inside and put his bottle in the sink. "He's here."

"Oh, Jesus." Louise closed the refrigerator with the rubber tip of her cane. "He's early."

Before he opened the front door Howard wiped his hands on his pants, pushed his hair back with two hands, and smoothed down his shirt.

The car pulled up to the house, and James Couch got out and stretched. He wore a thin white sweater and blue jeans; he was a short man with a white beard and a thick torso, and he was bald, the smooth dome of his head rising like something architectural. He came bounding up the steps and shook Howard's hand vigorously, nodding in time. His papery scalp stretched tight over the top of his head.

"Howard," he said.

"Hiya. Been a while."

"How've you been?"

"We've been okay."

"Louise's here?"

"You bet," Howard said. "Come on in."

James Couch leaned toward him and took his elbow, gently. Couch's white beard shone on his face; it was woven through with black hairs and looked infinitely soft. "I have something for you," Couch said.

"Okay."

"I'll give it to you later." Couch patted his pocket. "I want to see Louise first."

They went indoors and found Louise in the kitchen. She shook James Couch's hand. "You're a little early."

"Sorry," Couch said. "I didn't know where you were, so I gave myself some extra time. In case I missed a turn somewhere."

"Well. No harm done." She pressed his hand hard with both of hers. "We get lonely up here. We don't like to admit that, but it's true."

"We don't get lonely," Howard said.

"Yes, we do, Howard."

"No, we don't."

"It's beautiful up here," Couch said.

Louise smiled and widened her eyes. "Yes, it is. We forget about that sometimes. Come out on the porch."

They walked out to the porch together. The air was cool and smelled like dry grass and the dark, intricate depths of the woods. The mountains stood silhouetted against the green sky, and at the bottom of the pasture they could see the beehives, tall white boxes, luminous in the dusk.

Louise said, "It's hard to see it sometimes, when you see it every day."

Couch nodded, taking in the scenery. "You know, I went to Iceland this summer," he said. "Ever been there?"

"No," Howard said.

His wife said, "I suppose it's beautiful."

"Oh, hell yes. *Hell* yes. I was up there this summer, on vacation, you know, and what happens when I get there but there's this volcano going off, if you can believe it."

"Oh, for heaven's sake," Louise said.

"Yes. A thing to see. Steam everywhere. Lava going into the ocean, you know, really spectacular. You could see it for miles. Miles."

"What a coincidence," Louise said. "Good timing for you."

"Yes, it was. Yes, indeed." He reached into his pants pocket and took out a rock. It was an ordinary flat stone from the bottom of a river, smooth and black, with a white vein running through it. He gave it to Louise. "This is a piece of lava," he said. "From the volcano."

Louise took it, turned it over once in her palm. "Well," she said, "it's lovely."

"A brand-new rock. Five weeks old."

"*That* rock is?" Howard said.

"Howard," said Louise, "isn't it lovely?" She held it out to him; he took it from Louise's palm and felt it, heavy and cool, and handed it back to her.

"You got that in Iceland?" Howard asked. It was ridiculous. But Couch wasn't kidding.

"Keep it. I've got a dozen. We were living in the crater, you know. It was spectacular. Like being in the middle of a movie. Rocks flying everywhere."

"Living in the crater?" Howard said.

"Yep. For a month we lived in the crater. They had a motel there."

"A motel?"

"Yes, we were guests of the state. They needed volcano experts."

"You don't say," Howard said.

Louise turned the rock over. "It's very thoughtful of you," she said, and touched Howard's hand. "We'll put it in a special place. Thank you."

"It is my genuine pleasure." He smoothed his hand over his scalp. "I liked you guys a whole lot. You were the reason I stayed on at the ferries for as long as I did." He paused and then said, with great feeling, "*Iceland.*"

Far away, they could see a sprinkling of lights at the bottom of the hill; this was Roslyn, the town. Howard imagined what was happening there now, the pickups, the Dairy Queen full of teenagers. It was a pleasant thought, the idea of life going on elsewhere. He thought about James Couch, too, but it wasn't much of a thought, and it amounted to this: James Couch wasn't the man he had been. Or maybe that was putting it generously. Really what Howard thought, though he knew it wasn't polite, was this: James Couch had gone a little way around the bend, and he wasn't coming back.

At dinner, Louise said, "I don't remember you talking about your daughter."

"My daughter." Couch nodded. "My daughter is something to talk about. Now she — *she* is an adventurer." He ate normally, Howard noticed; he drank his beer out of a glass, which Howard himself never did. He didn't eat too quickly or too slowly. He chewed with his mouth closed. When he had food in his beard, he knew it, and wiped it away. He was handsome, Howard supposed, in a nautical way, with the beard and the sweater.

"What's your daughter's name?" Howard asked.

"Deedee. Deedee is a hang-glider."

"Is that so?" Louise said.

"Yes, it is. She's a daredevil."

"Good for her," Louise said.

"She goes up in the mountains and off she goes. Beautiful. She was telling me," Couch said, and pushed his chair back, "she got caught the other day in this updraft — she was over a hot spot, or however it is, you know, an upwelling — and she couldn't get out of it, and she kept going up, up, up, up." His flat hand rose slowly from the dinner table, tipping, and Howard watched it, entranced. "She couldn't do a thing. She just kept going up."

"Uh-oh," Howard said.

"You bet your life uh-oh."

Louise said, "It must have been terrifying for her."

"Well. So what happened was," Couch said, "she goes up and up, and just keeps going, and finally she goes out into outer space. Breaks right through the top of the atmosphere and she's just out there."

Howard cleared his throat. "In outer space?"

"My goodness," Louise said. "Imagine that."

"Luckily, she made it back," Couch said. "But she's sort of shied off the hang-gliding since then."

"I bet," Howard said.

"You can't blame her," Couch said.

"No, I guess not," Howard said.

"That must have been a wonderful trip," Louise said. "How beautiful, to be up so high."

"Like I say," Couch said, "she is an adventurer."

At some point during dinner, Louise squeezed Howard's knee once, hard, and smiled at him. Her hair was pinned behind her neck. She sat square to the table, with authority. She'd worked on the ferries for years, too, throwing out ropes, pulling them in, waving cars down the banging ramps.

When Couch went to the bathroom, Louise said, quietly, "So?"

Howard shrugged. "Got me."

"I don't think he should drive to Montana like that."

"Well, I don't know. He got here okay."

"I think he should stay with us tonight," she said. "We'll figure something out in the morning."

"Well," Howard said, "okay. We'll put him upstairs." They had a spare bedroom in the attic.

They sat together, listening to James Couch pee in the bathroom.

After a minute, Louise said, "You know, he's wonderful." She touched her fork, her knife. "I had no idea."

"I think what he is is crazy."

Louise lifted her arms into the air, embracing nothing. "I want to *keep* him," she said.

After dinner was cleared, they decided to watch the movies.

"This should be good," Louise said.

"Hell yes," James Couch said. "Put 'em on." He got up and began rearranging the furniture. Louise sat apologetically in her chair, not helping, every now and then taking a breath as though to speak. Couch in his white sweater lifted the living room chairs higher than he had to, and set them down with ostentatious care.

The strip of film was old, narrower than Howard remembered; it smelled flat and clean, like old tape. He threaded the film up and around, through the projector, and turned on the motor and the lamp. Immediately there was the hot smell of burning dust and the whirring sound of the film racheting through its rounds, curling up and around and gathering on the takeup reel.

Howard aimed and focused, and all at once, there he was on the white sheet on the wall, much younger, tragically younger, his face fuller and brighter, his arms stronger. His young hair whipped in the wind. He was on a ship, and behind him was a view of the sea, the open sea, and the ship was rocking slightly. But these weren't the ferry movies; these were his navy movies.

"These are the wrong movies," Howard said.

"That's all right."

"These are my navy movies. You won't recognize any of these people."

"Oh, that's okay. I don't mind."

"Well," Howard said, "that's Alaska." He found it difficult to speak. There he was. A group of men, their hair cut astronaut-short. They were tanned, shirtless. They waved. He was among them, the tall loose-jointed one in back, the one not wearing sunglasses. A boat was lowered into the water and motored away. Two men in wetsuits appeared from below the surface of the water and lifted their masks. A dark view of something that might have been a sunset.

He read the lid of the film can. "I guess this is 1957."

A mountain slid by, followed by a shot of the empty deck. Then a shot of the galley, where men squinted into the camera's obvious light, holding up their hands to shade their eyes. Another set of divers dropped abruptly into the water and sank.

"Daily life."

The screen went dark; next came a shot of the outside of their house in Seattle. The lawn was kept, as it always was: their old Plymouth sat at the curb, looking fierce and cantilevered, fins rising over the taillights.

"Oh, the Plymouth," Louise said.

Then Howard remembered this particular reel of film.

The wall went dark again. There was the inside of their Seattle house, the back hall. There stood the table, in its place; there was the old carpet, the old dark ceiling. Then, in the darkness, a figure appeared. It was Louise, naked, running from one doorway to another, the briefest of pictures. She was young and thin and almost all leg, or her legs were the brightest part of her, flashing when they scissored their way across the hallway and disappeared. Her torso was vaguer, darker. The shape of a small breast was fleetingly visible, the side of her face a smudge. But it was her.

The screen flashed a brilliant light, and the reel was over. Nobody said anything.

"Well," Louise said at last, thumping her cane on the carpet. "That would be me."

Howard turned on a floor lamp and switched off the projector. "Well, well," he said. He laughed, and Louise laughed, too. James Couch rubbed a hand over his bald head and tried to smile, but he couldn't manage it; he tipped his head to one side and looked at the floor. Howard remembered it now: he'd come home after three months, a sailor, and Louise had surprised him, appeared naked at the door, taken his bags, offered to make him coffee, all as if nothing were unusual. He'd taken the camera from his backpack, gone back outside, shot the house, the car, just as he had seen them, then used the last of the film on her. He felt a surge of real happiness at the memory. He was almost sixty-seven, she was sixty-eight, but it didn't matter. They had been together all their lives, or near enough. All this should have made him afraid, he thought, afraid of dying, but he wasn't afraid, not now, not on this hill, in this house. Nothing could make him afraid.

Louise, giggling, got up and turned on the dishwasher. Howard put the film chastely back into its tin container. Outside, the wind began to blow. Couch sat still for a moment longer; then he stood up and began putting the furniture back where it belonged. He reached up and unpinned the sheet, folding it once, twice, again, and hanging it over his arm, as a waiter would.

Howard opened the attic bedroom door. The roof sloped up to a peak; the walls were bare wood, dark old cedar. There was a white metal bed, a white dresser, an oval rug, all undisturbed for months. Above the bed was a small rectangular window, about the size of a magazine, giving a view on darkness. It was cold in the room, but there were blankets.

"This should hold you," Howard said, and took blankets off the dresser.

James Couch nodded, watching him placidly. "I really appreciate this," he said.

"That's a long drive you've got tomorrow."

"I know it."

"You need your sleep."

Couch helped spread the blankets over the bed. Then he said, "I can hardly remember us from before."

Howard tucked in the blankets. "We're just getting older."

"Maybe so."

Howard fluffed Couch's pillows. "If there's anything you need," he said when he was done, "just knock on our door. You know which one it is."

"Okay."

"There's only the one bathroom."

"That's okay. I can manage."

Howard couldn't think of anything more to say, but he didn't want to go. He stood for a while, watching Couch rearrange the pillows and smooth out the top of the blankets. At last he said, "Maybe you'll think about staying on tomorrow. I wouldn't mind at all."

"I've got to get back on the road."

"You'll stay for breakfast, at least. I'll show you my beehives."

"Sure. I'd like that." Couch felt his white beard and sat down on the bed. He began taking off his shoes. "I really do appreciate this," he said again.

"You bet. Any time." When Howard left him, James Couch was sliding his shoes carefully under the bed, first one, then the other.

Downstairs, Howard washed his face with an old thin washcloth. The cloth came away gray, and his hands, when he washed them, ran gray water down the sink. The wind had increased and now blew with some force across the chimney top. The house in its stand of trees was shut up tight, locked, and Louise was down the hall, in bed. Howard turned out the kitchen light. Conscious of his footsteps on the cold floor, he stepped softly, though he couldn't think why. From beneath their bedroom door a crack of light showed; Louise looked up from her book when he came in. Her hair hung over her shoulders. Howard loosened his belt and slid his pants to the floor. He opened one of the windows above their bed. In the back yard the fir trees bent as air swooshed through them. He'd spent so many years on the water, he thought.

Louise said, "Come to bed."

He climbed under the covers.

Louise kept reading. He turned on his bedside light and picked up a magazine. He read for a while, listening to the wind and feeling it on his cheek, a little too cold. Their feet touched under the blankets and moved apart again.

"He's okay?" she asked.

"He's okay."

She said, after a minute, "The poor man."

Howard listened for noise from the attic, but there wasn't any.

"He must have been wonderful," she said.

"You don't remember him?"

"No," she said.

Outside, the wind kept moving toward them over the fields, up the valley, and it filled Howard's heart as though his heart were a sail. Needles fell from the trees to the earth. The magazine fluttered in Howard's hands, turning its own pages.

After a while, Howard said, quietly, "You know I played the greatest concert halls in Germany before the war."

Louise turned a page. After a moment she said, "I never knew that."

"I ran in the highest circles of power," he said. "I was master among men."

"Oh, Howard," she said. "I had no idea."

"Ten thousand women waited on my every need."

"Really," she said.

"My name in lights around the world."

"Imagine," she said.

"Think of me like that."

"Yes."

"I flew in the great dirigibles of the age," said Howard.

"Yes, you must have."

"Flew over all the great nations of the earth."

"Yes, I know."

"Rivers and plains beneath me."

"Yes."

"It's true," Howard said. "Everything is true."

"Oh, Howard," Louise said, and closed her book. "Howard."